Karen Cushman

# RODZINA

A YEARLING BOOK

Published by Yearling, an imprint of Random House Children's Books
a division of Random House, Inc., New York

Yearling and the jumping horse design are registered trademarks of Random House, Inc.

Visit us on the Web! www.randomhouse.com/kids

Educators and librarians, for a variety of teaching tools, visit us at
www.randomhouse.com/teachers

ISBN: 0-440-41993-X

Reprinted by arrangement with Houghton Mifflin Company

Printed in the United States of America

March 2005

10 9 8 7 6

I WAS TEN YEARS OLD when Grandma Lipski took me to the Polish Cemetery in Chicago to show me her mother's grave. In front of a gravestone marked *Rodzina Czerwinski* she sat and cried, while I watched her, this tough little grandma who never cried.

Many years later, when I thought about writing a book about a Polish girl from Chicago, I decided to call her Rodzina after my great-grandmother. I checked with my father to make sure I had the spelling correct, and I discovered that Rodzina was not her first name, but was the Polish word for "family." The gravestone marked the resting place of the *rodzina Czerwinski*, or Czerwinski family.

*Rodzina* is about the search for a family, and I decided that while Rodzina was not my great-grandmother's name, it was the perfect name for the girl in my story. And so she is Rodzina.

I would like to dedicate this book to my family—the Czerwinskis, the Cushmans, and the Lipskis, who were kings in Poland.

# CONTENTS

# ❦ 1 ❦

# CHICAGO, 1881

ON A COLD MONDAY MORNING in March, when a weak, pale sun struggled to shine and ice glistened in the cracks in the wooden street, a company of some twenty-two orphan children with stiff new clothes and little cardboard suitcases boarded a special railway car at the station near the Chicago River. I know, because I was one of them.

The station was noisier and more confused than Halsted Street on market day. Travelers carrying featherbeds and bundles wrapped in blue gingham cloth shoved me aside in their hurry to get here or there. A man in a bright red jacket bumped into me and apologized in a language I did not know. At least I assumed it was an apology, because of all the bowing and tipping of his hat, so I said, "It's all right, mister, but I'd say you should know a little English if you expect to get wherever you're going." He tipped his hat again.

One woman, burdened with children, blankets, a tin kettle, and a three-legged stove, finally put that stove right down on the platform, sat herself atop it, and began to cry. I knew how she felt. I myself was a mite worried—not scared, being twelve and no baby like Evelyn or Gertie to be afraid of every little thing, but worried, yes. It was all so loud and disorderly and unfamiliar.

I forced my way through the crowd and grabbed on to a belt in front of me. The boy it belonged to said, "Hang on tight, Rodzina, afore we're swept into the lake like sewage." It was Spud, whom I knew from the Little Wanderers' Refuge. He and Chester, Gertie, Horton, Rose and Pearl Lubnitz, the baby Evelyn, and I—we had been there together. The others were from the Infant Hospital and the Orphan Asylum near Hyde Park. Orphans, all of us, carrying all we owned in our two hands, pushing and shoving like everyone else.

A lady, standing straight and tall in a black suit and stiff white shirtwaist, put her hands up to her mouth and shouted, but I could not hear much over the din. I finally gathered that she was from the Orphan Asylum and was calling us all together. Letting go of Spud's belt, I stretched myself even taller so I could get a better look at her over that expanse of heads. She was pale and thin, her mouth ill-humored, and her gray eyes as cold and sharp as the wire rims of her spectacles. I should have known they would not send someone kind and good-natured to accompany a carload of orphans.

Roaring and cursing, a short, barrel-shaped man togged out in a checked jacket and yellow shoes pushed his way through the crowd. "You! Orphans!" he shouted, the cigar in the corner of his mouth waving and waggling with his words. "Pipe down! I am Mr. Szprot, the placing-out agent for the Association of Aid Societies. That means I am the boss and you do what I tell you. You are, you know, none of you, too young to go to Hell. Or to jail. So shut your mugs and line up." After my time on the street I was used to being threatened with Hell, so it didn't bother me much, but still I shut my mug. There was silence from the other orphans too, and we walked noiselessly to the train.

Trains had hooted and rumbled behind our house on Honore Street, but I had never seen a locomotive up so close, looming like the fearful dragon of Wawel Hill in the story Auntie Manya used to tell, its smokestack belching sparks, and a line of cars trailing behind like a tail of wood and iron. If I had been younger or smaller, even I might have been scared.

Getting on this train had not been my idea. I wanted to go home. But I had no home anymore, except the Little Wanderers' Refuge, and they had sent me away to be sold as a slave. I knew that because a kid on the street, Melvin, had told me. "That orphanage ships kids on trains to the west," he said. "In freight cars. Don't feed 'em or nothin'. Sells 'em to families that want slaves." He shook his head. "Orphans never come to no good end." I found that easy to believe, so I believed every word.

No, I surely did not want to get on the train, but the crowd of orphans shoved me onward. The long black wool stockings they'd given me at the orphan home itched something fierce, and pausing midway up the iron steps, I bent down to scratch my knees. Three orphans knocked right into me.

"You, Polish girl," said Mr. Szprot, his voice even louder than his jacket, "try not to be so clumsy."

A big boy behind me snickered. "Clumsy Polish girl," he said. "Ugly cabbage eater." Accidentally on purpose I swung my suitcase and cracked him on the knee. I knew he wouldn't try to get even with Mr. Szprot so close.

Once up the steps, I looked back. This was the last I'd ever see of Chicago, this view of soot and ice and metal tracks. On such a cold, gray, blustery morning, it looked like a dead place, but at least it was familiar. Chicago had always meant Mama and Papa and the boys. Now Mama and Papa and the boys were gone, home was gone, and soon Chicago would be gone. I felt like I was jumping out a seventh-story window, not at all sure someone was down below to catch me. I scratched my knees again and, holding tight to my suitcase, went in.

The railroad car had ten or so rows of hard wooden benches lined each side of a center aisle. At the front was a potbellied woodstove for heat, which made the car smoky and stuffy but not very warm. There were, of course, windows, but I soon found that the open windows did not close and the closed windows did not open. In the back was a bucket of water, a dipper, and the toilet compartment. Less comfortable than the Little Wanderers' Refuge, I decided, but better than a Michigan Avenue doorway. I knew, for I had slept in both.

The car was so smoky that I shoved my way to an open window, knocking over Spud and a little girl with a runny nose as I did so. In front of and behind me were kids scuffling and shouting as they too fought for a window seat.

I pushed my suitcase under my seat. All I had in the world was in that suitcase: Mama's red-and-yellow shawl, the statue of the Virgin brought all the way from Poland, a big blue marble with a heart of fire that had belonged to Jan or Toddy—I never knew which—and a handmade card from Hulda that said "Friends 4-ever." On my feet were Papa's boots, which I'd worn since last autumn, when I left mine somewhere while I warmed my feet on the sun-soaked wood of the street. Everything else had been sold to bury Mama.

Mr. Szprot took his hat and jacket off and threw them on one of the seats. "Pipe down, you raga-muffins," he said, little blue veins popping right out on his egg-bald head with bad temper. "You should be grateful for this opportunity to be made into clean and useful men and women. It may be your last chance. So sit down, sit still, and thank God for your good fortune." The cigar in his mouth wobbled as he spoke, its ash growing longer and longer but sticking right there.

Finally we were all sitting, suitcases at our feet, our backs straight, proper and quiet. A tiny girl I did not know sat next to me. We sat there in silence for more than an hour waiting for them to load the rest of the cars.

When at last the conductor sang out, "All aboard!" a great crowd of people came running to the train, including a nun, who dragged two small, bedraggled-looking boys behind her. She stuck her head, white wimple and starched wings and all, in the window to talk to Mr. Szprot, and the boys commenced pushing and shoving each other, bellowing "Did so" and "Did not." I recognized them from my days on the street—Joe and Sammy, blond as broom straw and so skinny they were just bones held together by dirt. Joe was like a wild thing, angry and intense; Sammy was a more ordinary boy but always quick to disagree. Put them together and there was bound to be a fight.

The nun shoved Joe and Sammy on board and ran off, fearful, I think, that Mr. Szprot would change his mind about taking them. I never saw a nun run before. Her black robe billowed like the sails of a ship, and rosary beads swung from her waist. It was a spectacular sight.

"Rodzina, you old potato nose!" Sammy said, leaning over to punch my arm. "Ya got pinched too?"

I nodded. "A Holy Joe picked up a bunch of us kids and took us to an orphan home. But the home didn't want me and dumped me on this train."

"Aww, it won't be so bad. At least we'll eat regular. Just try to leave some potatoes for the rest of us," he said with a snicker.

Joe pushed him. "Get yer bones movin'!" Sammy pushed him back, and so it went until the bespectacled lady separated them and moved them along again.

They'd been eating potatoes the first time I saw them. I had just buried Mama and left our house on Honore Street, and I had no place to go. Walking through cold and windy Chicago in a coat too small and boots too big, I saw a small fire in the doorway of a church on Michigan Avenue, ringed by a crowd of children, big and small and in between, all dirt and sores and hunger. One boy, who had newspaper wrapped around his feet instead of shoes, looked a bit like my brother Toddy. "Can you tell me," I asked him, "where to get something to eat? I am awful hungry."

Some of the other children jeered, but the boy who looked like Toddy said, "Come on. Git yer feet under the table." I squatted next to him; he scooped a potato out of the embers of the fire.

"Hey," said the boy I later knew as Sammy, "look at her. She ain't hardly likely to starve, and I could sure use that potato."

"No, me," said Joe, grabbing at it. "Give it here, Potato Nose."

"Knock it off, you runts," said the boy who looked like Toddy, and he put the potato firmly into my hands. It smelled so good and felt so warm, I didn't know whether to eat it or just hold it. In the end I did a bit of both.

I wished I had a potato now, hot and crusty from the fire. Or a cup of soup with chicken, or . . . A whistle blew. With a great burst of steam and the squealing of iron wheels on iron rails, the train began to move. There was a rush of passengers who had to hop aboard, but no one jumped into our car. No one wanted to be an orphan. No one wanted to be packed into a railroad car like a flour sack and sent west to an unknown future, an enterprise I could not help but think would turn out badly, like everything else in our lives. No, no one wanted to be an orphan, including us orphans, only we had no choice.

Sparks, soot, and dust poured in, and everyone who had succeeded in getting an open window now fought and punched for a closed one. It was as if the entire car was full of Joes and Sammys.

I snatched up my suitcase, jumped over the little girl who shared my bench, and grabbed a seat right in front. Smoky as it was so near the stove, I had the seat all to myself.

I took off my coat and pressed my face against the window, snatching every last glimpse of Chicago that I could. I imagined Mama running after the train, the fringe on her shawl dancing in the wind. "Come back, Rodzina," she would call. "It was all a mistake. Come back. We are waiting for you at the house on Honore Street."

A small body came and shoved itself against me. "Kin I sit here with you?" said a girl with red hair pulled back into a braid as thick as my arm and a face like a holy angel. "I'm fearful scared."

Radishes! I sighed loudly to show I did not welcome company and stared at the sights out the window, which weren't much, being just more city and railroad tracks, then swamps and frozen prairie, for a long ways out of the station.

Finally the train picked up speed, and my whole world seemed to be jolting, swaying, bouncing, and jerking, and the constant noise of whistles and wheels and squealing brakes. We raced past scenes I had never seen before: houses surrounded by miles and miles of dark fields, cows and horses, rivers and creeks of clear icy water. Where were the grocers, the peddlers, the saloons, the churches and garbage dumps and apartment houses? Where did people buy their bread and block their hats? Where *were* the people? I might as well have been on the moon.

The intruder next to me interrupted with a gentle tap on my arm. "What's your name?" she asked.

I gave her the mean look I call the stink face, hoping it would discourage her questions.

She was maybe seven years old, pretty, tiny and delicate, with hair the color of spice cake and a smile so sweet, I knew everyone who saw her loved her. Me, I hated her. I was big, big for twelve and every day getting bigger, nearly tall as Papa, who was very tall, and round as Mama, who was very round.

I had not grown up wanting what I did not already have, except for one thing. I wanted to be pretty. When I told Mama, Mama said, "Pretty is as pretty does, Rodzina." Auntie Manya said, "What is this pretty? You got big hands, strong back, good teeth. What more you need?" Papa just smiled and said, "You are better than pretty. You look like me."

The girl nudged me again. "My name is Lacey. What's yours?"

"Rodzina Clara Jadwiga Anastazya Brodski," I said, not looking at her. I didn't want this girl to think we could be friends or anything. I just wanted to be left alone.

"I don't think I can remember all that. I'll call you Ro."

"Don't call me Ro. My name is Rodzina."

"Mine's only Lacey. That's all. Just Lacey. I'm a orphan."

*So who in this car ain't?* I thought.

I could feel my lip tremble but was resolved not to cry. Crying solved nothing. I had cried the day Mama died. For a long time afterward I cried, sitting on the shabby wooden stoop of our shabby wooden house, tears freezing in my eyelashes and my ears so cold they ached. I cried for Mama, newly dead of the putrid fever. I cried for Papa, killed at the stockyards by a runaway horse and buried in the great Sacred Heart Cemetery at Twelfth and Madison; for my brothers, long dead in a fire; for Hulda and Auntie Manya, gone away who knows where. But most of all I cried for myself. I was alone, hungry, and miserable. I could not remember being all those things before, leastwise not all at the same time. Papa and Mama had always been there, familiar and safe, with hugs and bread and cabbage. But now I was an orphan, and alone, and crying would not change that.

I said nothing more to Lacey but turned to look out the window. When I looked down at her after a while, she was fast asleep, eyelids twitching and thumb in her sweet, silly mouth.

For a time I watched out the window some more, wondering at all the land and sky. It was so different from Chicago. I already missed Chicago. I missed the smokestacks and the factories, the wash drying on the lines behind a hundred little houses, the sound of horse trolleys, and the smell of roasting nuts. I missed Mrs. Bergman, who lived downstairs with her twelve children; the grease man who traded grease for soap; and the Polish butcher, whose shop smelled invitingly of fresh meat and sawdust.

If I had to be an orphan, I would have chosen to stay at the Little Wanderers' Refuge. I had been often cold there, always hungry, nagged and scolded and held captive, but at least I was still in Chicago and had a bed off the street. But they did not keep children permanently—just until new homes were found. I was there only a few nights, long enough for a cold bath and an argument.

"I'm not going to be shipped west on a train like some sack of potatoes," I told Miss Hoolihan, as she buttoned me into my new dress.

"Yes, indeed, you are, and you're lucky to have the opportunity. Do what you are told, smile engagingly, and you will have a new home before Easter," she said.

"I do not want a new home. I want my mama and my papa back."

"We cannot work miracles."

Didn't I know that. "If I cannot stay here, I will live on the street again. I am old enough to take care of myself."

"You can't do that. You're only twelve."

"I'm big for my age."

"And stubborn for your age as well, but still you're only twelve, and we are responsible for you. So you will go with other orphans and travel west to a new home."

Who out there would want scruffy orphans from the streets of Chicago anyway? Only someone who wanted to work us to death, I'd say, just like Melvin told me. And if nobody took me, would I have to ride back and forth on this train, east to west and west to east, like some Eternal Traveler, giving rise to the legend of Rodzina the Unwanted, and have my story told around fireplaces, kitchen stoves, and campfires to scare little children? Either way I was mighty unhappy.

I went to the toilet at the back of the car. Through the hole in the seat I could watch Illinois race by. Miles and miles of Illinois.

Back in my seat, I bounced and nodded until the rhythm of the train and the whirling of my thoughts had me asleep. When I woke, Mr. Szprot was passing around red jelly sandwiches and apples from the big baskets in the back of the car. Lacey was still sleeping so I took hers too. I ate the sandwiches slowly, letting the sticky sweetness tickle my tongue, but I left Lacey an apple.

"Miss Brodski," I heard someone call. I looked around and there at the back of the car sat the lady from the Orphan Asylum, nodding her head at me. I took myself over there.

"Yes, miss?" I asked.

She frowned, her gray eyes as cold as a February fog off the lake. "It's Doctor."

"Doctor?" I had never heard of a lady doctor. "Really?"

"Never mind. Sit down," she said, pointing to

the seat next to her. I sat. She smelled faintly of soap and freshly ironed clothes. "There are more of you children on this train than we expected. Mr. Szprot is in charge of the older boys, but I am responsible for all the rest, and I cannot do it by myself. So I will take care of the babies," she said, nodding at a heap of children of maybe two or three sleeping all nestled together on the wooden benches in front of her, "and you will look after the other children: Horton, Gertie, Chester, Spud and Mickey Dooley, Sammy and Joe, and Lacey there, who is sitting by you. I will depend on you to see that they are clean, fed, quiet, and in the right place at the right time."

*Psiakrew*—dog's blood—as Auntie Manya used to say. I just wanted to be left alone. "Why me?"

"Because you are the oldest."

Old enough to be in charge of orphans but not old enough to be on my own? Didn't make much sense to me. I wanted to say, "Depend on someone else and leave me alone," but I didn't. I didn't want her to hate me, just let me be. I said only, "Yes, miss."

"Doctor," she said, looking down at the book in her hands.

I turned to go back to my seat and ran smack

into someone standing in the aisle. "I beg your pardon, as the convict said to the judge," said a skinny boy with a pale, freckled face. Both of his ears stuck out, his front teeth were missing, and one of his soft brown eyes gazed up to Heaven while the other looked up and down his nose.

"Who are you?" I asked, watching his eyes travel here and there, back and forth, never lighting for a moment on anything.

"Mickey Dooley, at your service," he said, sweeping off his brown wool cap to expose a crop of orange hair. Real orange. Carrot orange. "Orphan, purveyor of blarney, and a genuine bag of laughs. Nice to meet you." He pointed out the window. "And speaking of meat, holy moley, look at them sheep!"

A gang of boys standing behind him crowded around the window. "Them's not sheep; they's buffalo," said Joe.

"Moose!" said tubby Chester, smiling his crooked smile.

"Antelope!" Spud cried, his headful of yellow curls bouncing.

Having lived near the stockyards almost all my life, I knew cows when I saw them but did not choose to join the discussion. I might have to tend these kids, but the lady doctor didn't say anything about my setting them straight. I stumbled up the aisle and flopped into my seat.

At suppertime the train stopped. Some folks got off to eat. Us, we had more jelly sandwiches and apples. It wasn't pig's foot jelly or meat dumplings or sweet cake with raisins, but it was food. My stomach growled like an angry dog. You could hear it right out loud, it had gotten that quiet in the train car, except for the gurgling of Mickey Dooley's laughter and Gertie whining about how her elbow hurt or her toe or knee or someplace. The rest of us sat silently with our hunger, uncertainty, and jelly sandwiches.

Lacey was asleep again, so I finished my sandwich and half of hers and put the apples away in case I was hungry later. I knew I would be. I was always hungry. I loved food. Papa used to say, "Poles are the only people who write love poems about food." Were I a poet like my papa, I would write about cabbage rolls in tomato sauce, pickled herring, and the jelly doughnuts we ate each year on Paczki Day.

After supper the train got under way again. I washed hands and faces and helped Horton and Gertie blow their drippy noses. Because of my brothers I had plenty of experience with drippy noses and other details of child minding, but that didn't mean I had to like it. I must say, I didn't exactly hate it either. I was good with little kids.

The lady doctor and I got blankets down from the luggage racks and passed them out, for the car had grown colder. The other orphans huddled together for warmth, curling around kids they would have ignored in the light of day. Some cried out in nightmares, others whined or grumbled. I sat silent, wrapped in an itchy green blanket.

The gas lamps flickered in the darkness, making shadows dance on the walls and windows of the car. Once Papa's pants froze on the clothesline back of our house and he made them dance like a puppet. Back in the early years, this was, when he used to laugh and make jokes, before he found there was no place in Chicago for a Polish poet.

"Americans," he said, heading out one morning to his job at the stockyards, "are not a book-reading people." I sighed at the remembering and fell asleep, rocked by the jiggling and swaying of the train.

# ❧ 2 ❧

# SOMEWHERE IN
# ILLINOIS OR IOWA

THE STILLNESS WOKE ME shortly after dawn. The train had stopped. I could see some faded wooden buildings and a water tank and hoped this pathetic place wasn't the west.

It wasn't. Just a little town where the train had stopped for water. Some women in checked aprons and muddy boots got on, selling milk and small cakes, which Mr. Szprot bought for our breakfast, but not enough if you ask me.

I gathered the little girls for a trip to the water bucket to rid them of the breakfast still smeared on their hands and faces. As we passed the lady doctor's seat, the train started with a lurch and Gertie stumbled, grabbing at the lady to keep from falling down. "Don't touch!" she shouted, shoving Gertie's hand away. Radishes! Such a fuss over a little milk and cake on her skirt.

I helped Gertie stand back up, straightened her hair and the bow on her pinafore, and started to shepherd her back to the water bucket.

Then she, old Miss Don't Touch, said, "Rodzina—"

I stopped, letting Gertie go on without me. I was used to people saying my name the wrong way, but I wanted to give Miss Don't Touch as hard a time as she'd given Gertie. "That's pronounced *Rodzina*," I interrupted, making that sound between a D and a G and a Z that it seemed only Polish mouths could make, sort of like the G-sound in *bridge* or *cage* or *huge,* but not quite. The lady doctor sounded like a bumblebee with her Rod-zzzzzz-ina.

"Isn't that what I said, *Rodzina?*"

"No, you said *Rodzina.* It should be *Rodzina.* Like this: *Rodzina.*"

She looked at me like I was a hair in her soup. "I shall just call you Miss Brodski."

She pronounced that just fine. I thought to tell her, "That's *Brodski,*" and pronounce it exactly as she had, just to discombobberate her, but I didn't want to push my luck, so I nodded.

"Miss Brodski, you must do a better job of keep-

21

ing these children neat, quiet, and away from me."
She took a starched handkerchief from her pocket
and began to scrub at the stain on her skirt. "I have
enough to do with the babies. Now go."

I washed milk and crumbs off little faces with
the water in the bucket, scrubbing a bit roughly, I
must admit, but it was not my choice to be doing
this. After the children were settled in their seats
again, I sat down to suffer another day of swaying
and rocking. I could see nothing out the window
but more Illinois or Iowa or wherever we were.

Lacey visited the toilet and, after a while, came
skipping back to her seat, with Spud, Sammy, and
Joe trailing behind her. "Oh, Ro," she called.

"Rodzina," I said.

"We was looking out the window at horses," she
said. "I saw all different kinds. Black ones. And
black-and-white ones. And a brown one. And a
baby one." She bounced in her seat a few times. "I
hope we see a mo."

"A what?"

"A mo. You know, what you get mohair from.
Like for ladies' coats."

"Who told you that?"

"Spud. He said you get horsehair from horses
and mohair from mos."

The boys began to laugh and stomp their feet.

"And you are dumb enough to believe him?" I asked her.

Her eyes filled with tears. "I'm not dumb. Just slow. Them folks at the Infant Hospital said I was just slow and plumb fine to go west and work for my keep."

Spud shouted, "Yeah, she's so slow, she makes molasses look fast."

"Slow as a broken clock," said Sammy.

"Slower than a dead turtle," added Joe.

They stomped their feet again and hooted with laughter.

"What exactly do you mean, slow?" I asked Sammy.

"You know. Feebleminded."

I drew back. It was bad enough to share my seat with Lacey and wash her sticky face, but now she turned out to be feebleminded. Did they expect someone would want a feebleminded orphan?

The only feebleminded person I had ever known was Noodlehead Weber, who swept the floor at the candy store. Some of the kids threw rocks at him, but Mama wouldn't let me. She was always nice to him and made me call him Clarence and never Noodlehead.

I reckoned Mama would want me to be nice to this little girl and not call her Noodlehead or laugh at her. *I promise, Mama, but don't expect we're going to be friends or anything.*

"I ain't feebleminded!" Lacey shouted, her little face turning from pink to bright red. "Just slow."

I said, "Seems to me some people are feebleminded and some are plain ugly. Like them." I pointed to the boys. "Just be grateful you ain't them."

"I ain't ugly," said Joe, standing up and waving clenched fists in my face.

"Sammy," I said, "make your brother behave."

"Joe ain't my brother," Sammy said.

"I don't care. Just keep him quiet."

Lacey and I sat back, lost in our own thoughts. The boys jostled and snickered for a while longer and then got bored with that. They sat down on the floor, warming their backs by the stove, and Spud pulled a deck of cards out of his pocket. They started up a poker game, betting peach pits and marbles instead of money. Also James A. Garfield campaign ribbons, empty thread spools, broken spectacle parts, and anything else they found in their pockets. I guess the betting was more fun than the poker, for soon I heard Sammy call out, "Reckon I kin hold my breath longer than any fella on this here train."

And Joe said, "Bet you there are at least fifty flies stuck on that flypaper."

"I could count to a hundred before we see another tree, I wager," Chester shouted, coming to join the others, and more marbles and junk changed hands. I think someone could have been found to bet on whether or not the sun would set that night.

The gamblers shouted and squealed, their ruckus accompanying the squealing, jangling, and tooting of the train in an awful sort of music that sounded like a brass band played by monkeys.

A skinny old conductor came in to check the stove, his big, fuzzy ears sticking way out from under his peaked cap. He whistled while he worked. I got up and went over to him. "How long," I asked, "will it take to get to Grand Island?" Miss Hoolihan had said that would be the first orphan stop.

"Oh, three or some days," he said, scratching one of his huge ears, "depending on how often we got to pull over to let an express train go by. A little longer if we run into train robbers or a blizzard or a prairie fire, if we run off the rails or a bridge is washed out, or some such."

Train robbers? Washed-out bridges? Blizzards and prairie fires? Was he pulling my leg or were we really facing such dangers? He tipped his cap to me and whistled himself off.

What was I doing here? Was it a punishment for being an orphan? There were days and days of this misery ahead—noise and swaying and rattling and worrying. I would not survive. *I will lie right down here in this aisle,* I thought, *and die of swaying and rattling and washing up. And there will be no one to mourn for me.* I was almighty blue.

I rocked and stumbled back to my seat. Lacey was eating an apple. She gave me a scared smile.

"Are we almost there?" she asked.

"Where?"

"Wherever we're going."

"We're going lots of places, but we ain't at any of them yet," I said.

As I watched the land rush by, the skies grew darker and darker. A flash of light preceded the sound of thunder. Mickey Dooley shouted, "Put the frog out, Bill. I think it's gonna rain!" And it did. It rained cats and dogs. Walking sticks and flowered hats. Plum cake and sausages, fishbowls and fur-lined caps. Washed-out bridges and prairie fires and who knows what else.

Thunder rolled in once more, and lightning danced in the sky. Screaming and trembling, Lacey pulled her skirt up over her head. I turned away from her. Being scared, like having lice, was something one was supposed to keep to oneself.

The gamblers turned to racing raindrops, cheering them on, betting on which would be first to reach the bottom of the window. Marbles and peach pits changed hands again.

"Hey, Potato Nose, want to get in on this?" Sammy asked. "Try your luck?"

I shook my head. I had plenty of luck—all of it bad. If I wagered with them, I'd no doubt lose my boots, my hair, and my seat on the train and end up bald and barefoot, lost on the prairie. No sir. Not me. I would not bet on anything good happening for me.

When the rain finally eased, I could see only flat fields and scattered black patches of plowed earth. Late in the afternoon, we passed the first house we had seen in some hours. Leaning on the fence was a boy who looked like he had been waiting for us. The engine tooted; he waved and then hung there until the train passed, even longer maybe. Maybe he's still there, waiting for us to come back.

*They should send some orphans to that kid*, I

thought. Never had I seen a face so lonely. I bet he'd be good to them and not make them work too hard, so grateful he'd be for their company. And at night they could pop corn and tell stories, and when the train passed by, they could all go wave to it together and then talk about it after supper.

As the light failed outside, the conductor lit the gas lamps. Mr. Szprot passed out jelly sandwiches again. And apples. And sticks of celery. I wondered what he and Miss Doctor ate. Did they have to be satisfied with jelly sandwiches like we did? I looked behind me to check. Mr. Szprot was snoring in his seat. Miss Doctor was occupied with the littlest kids, cutting up apples for them to share. Maybe she didn't eat at all. I wondered what had happened to her sandwich.

I stretched my feet out toward the stove, letting the heat defrost my toes. "I hurt," said a little voice in front of me. Gertie, of course.

"You ain't going to vomit, are you?" I asked, pulling away.

She shook her head. "But I hurt all over."

"Maybe you're just cold. Sit here by the stove a minute." She tried to climb into my lap, but I crossed my legs and settled her between Lacey and me.

The big boy who had called me Cabbage Eater swaggered over to warm his hands. "Hey, Herman," Sammy said from his seat across the aisle, "I remember you from Chicago."

"Call me Hermy the Knife," the boy said, fingering something in his pocket that might or might not have been a knife. He was one scary-looking fellow—what my mama would call a *chuligan*—with his greasy hair, crooked nose, and a shadow above his lip that just might be the beginnings of a mustache. "Yeah, I remember you. You and your brother."

"Joe ain't my brother," Sammy said.

"I thought you was happy in Chicago," said Joe. "How come you're on this train?"

Hermy shrugged. "I'm here, but I ain't sticking around. Taking off as soon as I get the chance. Don't want nothin' to do with no hicks, hayseeds, rubes, clodhoppers, yokels, or bumpkins."

"Don't you want a family?" Gertie asked Hermy.

"Don't need no family," said Hermy. "I got my gang, the Plug Uglies, and we don't let nobody push us around—especially some yokel from Yokelsville." At that Hermy the Knife stopped and noticed who was speaking to him. "Hey, it's Gertie the Whiner. And Cabbage Eater, and looky here, they're sittin' with Cabbage Head, who don't know how many beans make five. You three are just right for Yokelsville."

"Cabbage Eater! That how you got so big, eatin' cabbage?" asked Sammy.

"And don't forget potatoes—we seen her eat plenty of potatoes," Joe added.

"Yeah, *our* potatoes."

I turned and looked out the window again. Could *I* just take off like Hermy? I was old enough and big enough to take care of myself, but we weren't in Chicago anymore. Where were we? And where would I go from here?

I fell asleep but was awakened sometime later by the sounds of crying. That wasn't unusual in this car full of orphans, but this crying was right in my ear. Gertie. Of course.

"Shh, Gertie. Cuddle up with Lacey and go back to sleep."

But she kept crying, and the other kids began to stir. "Come with me," I said, pulling her by her hand to the back of the car.

The lady doctor was looking out the window. I couldn't see why—it was just darkness out there. Black darkness.

Gertie blubbered again and pushed her face into my skirt. "Miss," I said.

"Doctor," she said.

"Gertie here won't stop crying. And she's waking up all the other kids."

The lady doctor turned to us. "Leave her with me. I'll take care of her." The gaslight flickered on her glasses, shooting off sparks in my direction. I shivered, glad it was Gertie and not me left with old Miss Don't Touch.

# ❧ 3 ❧

# OMAHA

IT WAS STILL DARK NIGHT when we all had to wake, trudge off the train from Chicago with our suitcases, walk through the sleety Omaha railroad yard, and climb aboard the Union Pacific train that would take us the rest of the way to Grand Island. I stumbled as I walked, having gotten used to the rocking and swaying of the train. Our car looked just the same as the last, except that all the windows closed, so we were soon settled down again, I by the stove, Lacey next to me once more.

The night was quiet after that, except for the *rackety-rack* of the wheels and an occasional whistle, but I could not go back to sleep. I could see Mama's face there outside the window. And Papa's. And the boys, and Auntie Manya, and Hulda. Lacey reminded me a little of Hulda—she had the same thick braid of hair and rosy cheeks—but Hulda's hair was black as night and she wasn't feeble-minded. Hulda and I sat next to each other in school and took turns with a roller skate we found in the street until it broke in two. She swore we would be friends forever, but when her new step-mother began beating on her, Hulda ran away and I never saw her again. I had to leave school when I turned nine to help Mama with the little boys and the house and the sewing, and I never had another friend.

I felt a wave of loneliness, like I was all alone on this train. Just me and the dark night outside. I looked around. Everyone else was asleep. Every-one but grouchy old Miss Don't Touch in the back, who was watching out the window again. Was she better than no one? I sighed. I supposed she was. I walked back to her seat.

"Miss Don't— er, Doctor," I said, catching my-self just in time.

"Go to sleep, Rodzina."

"I can't sleep. I thought I could talk to you."

"I am busy."

"You aren't doing anything but looking out the window."

She looked at me. "And that is enough. You can wait until morning."

"It's now I can't sleep, Miss Doctor. Let me talk with you awhile, and then I will leave you to your looking."

She moved over and I sat down. "I been wondering," I said. "Do you go back and forth, back and forth, on this here train with orphans like Mr. Szprot does?"

"*This* is what could not wait until morning?"

"Miss Doctor, I am just trying to ease into a conversation." I scratched my knee and sighed.

She sighed too, and said, "Miss Brodski, I am not your mother or your friend. And having conversations with orphans in the middle of the night is not among my duties."

I could feel my face grow hot, but before I could respond, she continued, "I am employed by the Orphan Asylum to look after you orphans only as far as Wyoming Territory. Then I am free."

"And then?"

"Then I will join a circus and ride bareback. Or pilot a balloon around the world. Or marry a Vanderbilt. I have not yet decided. Now are you ready to sleep?"

Miss Doctor joking? Strange. But then strange

things happened in the middle of the night. Maybe she would really listen to me. It was worth a try. "Miss Doctor, I didn't want to come on this old train. I don't want to go live with strangers. Couldn't I just go back with Mr. Szprot to the orphanage and—"

"It is our job to find you a place to live."

"But I don't want—"

"It does not matter what you want. Do you think *I* want to be here? I am a doctor, not a nursemaid. But here I am. And here you are. Now go back to your seat."

Jeepers, she was no better at listening than a fruitcake. Why had I thought she would help me anyway? She was probably in cahoots with all those folks out there who took orphans to be slaves and beat them and starved them because no one cared whether they lived or died.

And where was Gertie? She was not with Miss Doctor, where I had left her before Omaha. So where was she? The stiff and starchy doctor lady had probably stuffed poor Gertie into a suitcase and left her by the tracks.

I slumped into my seat. Lacey was awake, looking at me with her big eyes glowing in the light from the gas lamps. "Where were you? I was plumb scared, and I don't like to be scared." Snuffling, she leaned up against my side.

Radishes! I pulled away. "Why are you bothering me? I don't want to be your friend or anything, but still you're always hanging on me."

Lacey pushed herself against me again. "I feel safer when you're here. You're so big and sturdy, like a beautiful tree I can lean on and not knock over."

A tree? What an odd thing to say. I figured she couldn't help it, being feebleminded, and I let her lean for a minute.

A beautiful tree. Was that a good thing or a bad thing? I wondered.

I pressed my face against the glass. Clouds hurried across the sky, and suddenly there was the moon, flooding the passing prairie with silver light, like the landscape in a fairy tale. My mama told me Moses found a man once gathering sticks on the Sabbath and banished him to the moon. And it is his shadow we see up there and call the man in the moon. I sighed. *I miss you, Mama. I wish you didn't leave me.* I knew Mama couldn't hear me. If there was such a place as Heaven, Mama was there already, telling God what to do and scolding the Virgin Mary for being too thin, she

36

should eat something. And I was alone. *I miss you, Mama.*

I watched out the window for a long while. It was growing light, but I could see no buildings, no trees, no bushes. It appeared Nebraska was all dead grass and endless sky, as far ahead as I could see, as far ahead as I could imagine.

At midday we passed a wagon train of emigrants going west. Plodding mules pulled great canvas-covered wagons packed with bedding and house-hold stuff. The children waved to us with their ragged straw hats, while women in calico gowns and sunbonnets just stood, watching us speed past.

The afternoon erupted into noisy restlessness. "Come over here, you sprouts," I said finally to Lacey and Joe and Sammy and Horton, Chester, Spud, and Mickey Dooley. And Gertie. No Gertie. Where was Gertie? I'd go look for her in a minute. "I will teach you to play Intery Mintery Cuttery Corn."

"Can Nellie and Kitty play too?" Lacey asked.

"Who?"

"Nellie and Kitty. They was at the Infant Hospital too. Nellie got brung because her ma's new husband didn't want her around. And Kitty's mama drinks."

I nodded. While Lacey went back to fetch Nellie and Kitty from Miss Doctor, I thought about how awful it would be to be on this train and not be an orphan. To be part of a family that didn't want you. No matter how poor we were or what trouble there was, I never felt that my mama and papa didn't want me. Why, they carried me all the way from Poland to Chicago with them so we could be together.

In Poland Papa had been a bookstore clerk, a poet, and a writer of angry letters to the editor of the newspaper, urging Poles to rise up against their German rulers. One night he clouted our German landlord right on the nose. I do not doubt the landlord deserved a clouting, but still Mama and Papa and I left Poland that night, with only a few hundred *złotys*, a featherbed, and a plaster statue of Panna Maria, the Virgin Mary. I heard of this from my papa. I do not remember it myself, for I was only two at the time, occupied with learning to walk and talk and not at all interested in politics.

While they lived, I was never unwanted. I never cried myself to sleep. I never went to bed hungry, although sometimes my stomach was full of nothing but potatoes. We may have slept three to a bed—

five when the boys were alive—but there was always a bed. And arms to hug me and someone to spit on a thumb and wipe the dirt from my chin. If only they had not died. . . . If only I could . . . If only . . .

Someone pulled my sleeve. "Come on, Ro. You said you'd teach us the corn game." So I did, and that was the end of remembering for a while.

When the train stopped for supper, those passengers in the other cars lucky enough to have coins in their pockets got off to eat. The eating station glowed with cheerful lights in the gathering darkness. Smells of frying meat and baking pies escaped from the kitchen and made their way to the orphan car. We orphans crowded into the seats on the station side, stuck our noses out the window, and sniffed.

"If I was eating there," said Spud from the seat in front of me, "I would have boiled pike with horseradish sauce and carrot soup."

"Roast beef for me," said Sammy, jumping up and down in his seat.

"No, pork sausage," said Joe.

"Hot white bread with butter," Chester added, "and roast chicken."

"Pie," Lacey whispered to me. "A lot of pie."

Mr. Szprot came then with our supper. Jelly sandwiches, of course, and cold potatoes, from those big baskets that seemed likely never to run out.

Mickey Dooley looked at his sandwich and said, "If we had ham, we could have ham and eggs . . ."

"Shut yer Irish mug, Dooley!" one of the big boys yelled.

". . . if we had eggs," Mickey finished, and laughed.

"Quiet, you thugs," said Mr. Szprot. "The doctor and I must step off the train for a moment. The babies are asleep, and I will send the bigger boys outside. You, Polish girl, watch over this crowd here and keep them on the train and quiet."

I had the suspicion Miss Doctor and the Szprot were going to the eating station for steak and beer. "Seems *they* don't have to live on jelly sandwiches," I said after they left.

"I bet they have corned beef and cabbage," Spud said.

"And chocolate cake," said Chester.

"And ice cream!" said Joe, jumping up.

I thought I'd better get their attention before there was a rebellion, with orphans rushing the eating place and grabbing all the food. "In Poland no one ever had to eat jelly sandwiches," I said as I chewed. "My mama always used to say, 'In Poland we had every meal cheese, butter, eggs, honey, carrots, and beer.'"

"What's Poland?" Lacey asked.

"It's another country, where I was born."

"Far away?"

"Very far."

"Did you have to take a train like this?"

"A train and a wagon and a ship with no light and no air and people packed close as beans in a can."

"Why did you leave Poland if it was so good there?" asked Sammy. "Not enough potatoes for you?" He snorted through his nose.

"We left because Papa said poor freedom was better than rich slavery."

I shook my head. Poor Papa. He found little freedom in Chicago, rich or poor. And little contentment. I think his happiest days were those Saturday afternoons when he did not work, when he and I would walk to the shops on Ashland Avenue. There we would buy supper: the spicy sausages called *kiełbasy*, freshly ground horseradish, cherries maybe, and a round rye bread. Papa would bargain to get the best prices, speaking German to the baker, Yiddish to the pickle man, even a little Italian to the greengrocer. He'd pay the Polish butcher whatever he asked, and then they would argue happily about Poland and politics until I'd pull on his sleeve, impatient to get home.

"All sorrows are bearable if there is bread," Mama said to me once as I handed her our supper.

"Papa says freedom is better than bread," I told her.

She narrowed her eyes. "The egg does not teach the hen. Go and get water for soup." So I trudged down three flights of stairs to the pump in the yard, filled the bucket, and carried it back three flights up. I did not argue with Mama again until my arms were not so sore.

Spud's sharp elbow poked into my side. "I asked you, can you talk Polish?"

"I can call for *klops* and *kapusta* to eat. And I can understand a little. That's about all." We always spoke English at home so Mama could learn, although until the day she died, her English sounded like Polish. "Oh, and I can say your names. *Świnia*," I said to Spud, *"Osioł"* to Joe, and *"Łajdak"* to Sammy.

I looked on, pleased, as the boys shoved and wrestled in their seat, calling each other Pig, Donkey, and Villain in Polish. And the names were too good for them.

Suddenly I remembered Gertie. "Anyone seen Gertie?" I hadn't seen her since taking her to Miss Doctor before we even got to Omaha.

"I ain't seen her," said Sammy. And Joe. And Chester and Lacey.

I searched the car. No Gertie sleeping on a bench, warming by the stove, whining out a window. Was she not on the train anymore?

Mickey Dooley came out from visiting the toilet in back. "Have you seen Gertie lately?" I asked him, getting mighty worried about losing her.

"I seen her with the doctor lady when we changed trains," said Mickey. "But not since. I don't think Gertie's on this train."

"Could Miss Doctor have just left her in Omaha?" We orphans all shook our heads. Was it her punishment for whining and soiling the lady's skirt? Poor Gertie. I hoped she was put in an orphanage and not just left on the railroad platform, but with Miss Doctor and the Szprot, one could never tell. I would have to watch my step for sure.

"I didn't want to come on this here train," I said, "but I sure wouldn't want to be dumped off just anywhere in the middle of the night."

"You didn't want to come?" asked Chester. "*I* sure did. They said I could grow mushmillions. I love mushmillions." Who didn't, I thought—all that sweet and juicy fruit. But I doubted Chester would ever even see a melon once he became a slave.

"They promised me a nice home," said Spud, "where I could drive horses and oxen and have as many apples and pears as I want to eat."

"The fellow from the Little Wanderers' Refuge said they'd give me a farm!" Horton added.

Mickey Dooley said, "They gave me my first pair of shoes in three winters, so here I am."

Boy, would those boys be disappointed when they saw who was taking them and for what awful purpose. I shook my head again.

Chester swallowed his last bite of sandwich and asked me, "If you didn't want to come on this train, why are you here?"

"What do you think, they paid me a hundred dollars? I'm here because I had nowhere else to go and was made to come." I was starting to regret being too friendly when I just wanted to be left alone. I turned and stared out the window as they talked on about shoes and farms and mushmillions.

Out the window in light from the moon I could see some of the big boys fooling around on the station platform, pushing each other and laughing and carrying on the way they did, the cigarettes they got who-knows-where glowing like little lanterns in the darkness. Hermy yelled, "All aboard!" and there came running everyone from the dining room, still with napkins tucked in their shirts, some with forks in their hands. The conductor came out and grabbed a couple of the boys by their ears. "Just a little prank, folks!" he shouted. "Ten more minutes. Go back and eat. We have ten more minutes." Most people went back in to finish their suppers, but not everybody, so anxious were they not to miss the train and be stuck in this place with nothing but an eating station and the moon.

# ❧ 4 ❧

# GRAND ISLAND

THE MORNING HAS GOLD in its mouth, Papa used to say. I understood as I woke to a flash of new-risen sun across the plains. All that day the country flew by in a blur of yellows and browns. I had not known the United States was so big, and the west so far away. Never had I been so far from home. Well, Poland was farther, I knew, but it was not my home, really, in that we left when I was too young to remember. Home was that room on the third floor on Honore Street, and it was miles and miles and miles behind me as we traveled into the unknown.

That evening as we sped toward Grand Island, farther into the great state of Nebraska, Mr. Szprot called us all together. "You ragamuffins, sit and be quiet." He waited, cigar wobbling up and down, four-inch piece of ash dangling off the end, until all twenty of us (well, twenty-one with all of us) were in our seats with our mouths closed before he went on. "Grand Island, as you know, will be your first opportunity to meet the ladies and gentlemen of the west who will be your new families." More accurately, the first time we would be paraded like cattle, sold as slaves, disposed of like old meat, I thought.

"I want to assist you all in landing good homes. You big boys," he said to Hermy the Knife and some others, "will be much in demand to help with farm work." Slaves. I knew it. "The rest of you must be at your most appealing." He grinned, cigar stuck between his yellow teeth. "Leastwise those of you who can be appealing. Now, watch me." He got down on his knees and crawled over to Sammy. "Please, sir, I want to go home with you," he said, a high, babyish voice coming from behind the cigar. "Please, could I go with you? I'm a good little boy." How could even folks as unfeeling as Szprot and the lady doctor send these little kids to be slaves to strangers? I turned away, disgusted.

While Mr. Szprot and the younger orphans practiced, Hermy the Knife flopped himself onto the seat next to me. "First stop, I'm cuttin' out of here, back home to Slabtown," he muttered. "I ain't goin' to work on no farm with no yellow-haired hayseed from Nowhere Town. No sir, not me." He turned and saw me next to him. "What you lookin' at, clumsy Polish girl? Immigrant. Greenhorn. Why don't you go back to wherever it is you come from?"

"I come from Chicago, just like you, lunkhead," I said.

He stood up, fire in his eyes and, I guessed, in his fists. He was awful big but stupid, whereas I was big, strong as an ox, and smart. I was not afraid of him. I stood up too.

There we were, near eye to eye, rocking and bouncing in that train, getting closer and closer to Grand Island. Finally Hermy said, "Greenhorn," spat on the floor, and shoved his way to the back of the car through the crowd of orphans pulling on each other and saying, "Please, could I go home with you and be your little boy?"

I sat down again. I would not practice. I would not beg to be taken by strangers and mistreated. I wanted to be left alone.

After more rocking and swaying and pleading, the rehearsal ended. Those few orphans who had a change of clothes put on their best duds. Most were like me; our old clothes had been discarded as worthless at the orphan home, and we stood, sat, and slept in what we had been given: plaid dresses and pinafores for the girls, knickers and jackets and ties for the boys—except for Sammy and Joe, who had come straight from the street in their dirty knickers and ragged shirts. After our days and nights on the train, the rest of us didn't look much better than they did.

I took off my pinafore, which appeared to have been the battlefield for a fight between a jelly sandwich and an ash can. The dress beneath was wrinkled and travel stained but would have to do.

Miss Doctor and I helped the little ones straighten their clothes. "Come here, Joe," I said. "Let me neaten you up a bit."

As I reached to tuck in his shirt, he pulled roughly away. "Keep yer mitts off me."

"Sammy, tell your brother—"

"Joe *ain't* my brother," Sammy said, but he moved in to fix Joe's shirt and slick down his hair.

"Now me, Ro," said Lacey.

"Rodzina," I murmured as I unbraided her hair. Now, my hair was all right—yellowish and a little wavy but ordinary. But Lacey's hair was gorgeous, almost alive, snapping and sparkling, standing out about her head like the halo around a streetlight on a foggy night. I could have hated her for her hair alone. I may have pulled a little harder than necessary as I brushed and rebraided it.

We rounded a sharp bend, and the train leaned way over. I saw Nellie grab Miss Doctor's skirt in her sticky hand and hold on tight. Frowning, Miss Doctor yanked her skirt away so hard, Nellie almost fell down. *Why is that lady doctor so frosty and unfriendly?* I wondered. Would it have killed her to be nice to us, orphans that we were? Why, doctors were as rich as cream. She was bound to have hundreds of skirts. So what if a little jelly got on this one? I feared Nellie would disappear like poor Gertie for the crime of touching Miss Doctor.

I waved Nellie over to me, dusted her off, and smoothed her hair. "Here," I said to her, "hang on to *my* skirt." She did.

Mr. Szprot got all us orphans together to practice our singing for tonight. Why folks would be so blamed eager to hear orphans sing I don't know, but it seemed to be so. Mr. Szprot stood in the front of the car, his cigar waggling and his hands waving around like he was drawing pictures in the air while we sang, loud and lively and out of tune. "Yankee Doodle" was my favorite, for Chester's voice broke each time on the last word—*han-dy*—and it was better than the whole rest of the song.

Singing made me warm, so I got myself a dipperful of water to wash my face and cool off. Mickey Dooley came over and asked, "Water you going to do with that?" but I ignored him. Did you ever notice how folks with the least to say talk the most? Take Mickey Dooley.

We passed more farms and less prairie. Then a clump of small wooden houses, shops, even a church. And there we were in Grand Island, which was neither grand nor an island, far as I could see.

The sun was setting as we stepped out of the train onto a tiny platform, and the sky was lit up like the Fourth of July—fluffy white clouds, bursts of gold, and flames of orange. Then darkness fell like a velvet cloak. Never had I seen such a sunset, and it clean broke my heart. I took a deep breath and then another and another. The air smelled so good, pure and clean, like nothing bad ever happened here. Not like Honore Street in Chicago, with its slaughterhouses, garbage dumps, and creeks bubbling with sewage.

We lined up on the platform. Miss Doctor had two of the littlest girls by the hand. "Rose and Pearl Lubnitz are going back home," Mr. Szprot told us. "Their mother changed her mind about giving them up and wants them back." He chewed his cigar a bit. "Better for them, I suppose. I find in general orphans come to no good end."

Miss Doctor frowned and nudged him. "While we go to engage someone to take them back to Chicago," he went on, "you alley rats stay right here."

We all watched them walk into the station. Lucky Rose and Pearl Lubnitz. You could hear sighs and whimpers and out-and-out crying from those left behind. I'd wager every one of us wanted a mama to go back to, someone who'd take us from this train and back to Chicago, where'd she'd say, "It was all a misunderstanding. I am not dead and you have not been sent away," and would make us pound cake and lemonade and tuck us into bed.

I shook my head and began to read the announcements pasted on the wall:

---

# Wife wanted by Western gentleman.
Must be clean, good cook, and have pleasant disposition. No children or annoying relatives. Write Henry Spurior, Moose Lick, Montana.

*Ha!* I thought. *That might be a good position for Miss Doctor, after she gets rid of us orphans, except for the part about "pleasant disposition."*

---

# MY SETS OF TEETH CANNOT BE BEAT!
Dr. Everett's PAINLESS Dental Parlor.
Teeth extracted positively without
pain by the use of Vitalized air.
— NO PAIN OR NO PAY —
Dentures 5.00. Perfect fit. Fillings 50 cents,
1.00 for gold. Ten years guarantee.
273 Merchant Street at Oak.
HOURS 830 AM to 8 PM,
Sunday 10 AM to 5 PM.
★ We are no Floating Dentists ★
WE ARE HERE TO STAY.

---

# WHEREAS SOME EVIL DISPOSED PERSON
or Persons is employed in Circulating
Scandalous reports injurious to the
Character of Mrs. Turk, No. 6 Miller Street,
whoever will give information of the
Offender or Offenders so that they may be
brought to Justice shall be handsomely
Rewarded for their trouble.

And here we were on the notice board, for sale
just like hair restorer!

---

The notice didn't say a word about selling us or giving us away for servants. It even sounded a bit like they cared what happened to us. But I knew better.

"Hey, Cabbage Eater, got any smokes?" Spud asked me. He grinned with his big, stickout teeth. "I'm dyin' for my coffee and smokes."

When I shook my head no, he moved on to join his pals, who were panhandling on the station platform. They asked, "Got a penny for an orphan?" of all those getting on and off the train or just lounging on the benches, waiting for something to happen. Unfortunately Spud asked, "Got a penny?" of a man in a checked coat before he noticed it was Mr. Szprot! Spud was rewarded not with smokes but with a smack and a shove back into line. I got a frown from Mr. Szprot.

Finally we all walked together to the schoolhouse. Papa's boots, being too big, rubbed and chafed my feet, and my knees itched something awful.

We were shown into a big room with a table full of pies and cakes on one side and rows of benches end to end on the other. While we climbed up on the benches so that folk could get a good look at us, I took a gander at them. There were some fifty or so men and women, looking the way I imagined farmers would look: weathered and tired, in faded cotton broad-brimmed hats and limp bonnets. They hadn't bothered to put on their Sunday clothes just for us.

What if one of them picked me? I did not want to go home with any of these strangers. I slouched behind the others so no one could see me.

After we sang a round or two of "There's a Light in the Window" and "Home on the Range," Mr. Sourfaced Szprot stood up. "I have the pleasure," he said, "of bringing before you a select group of Chicago's homeless waifs." He waggled his cigar a time or two. "Do not call them unfortunate children, for although without home and family, these children are fortunate indeed to have this opportunity to find good homes away from the ignorance, poverty, and vice in which they were found in Chicago."

He went on, but I was too angry to listen. I was not found in ignorance and vice, and no Mr. Sourface was going to talk so about my mama and papa. I could almost see them there before me, gentle Papa cradling a book in his big hands, Mama sewing flowers on hats late into the night for ten cents a dozen, Papa and Mama smiling as they swung me around in a Christmas Eve dance.

When Szprot finished talking, the farmers and their wives walked by, looking at us like we were puppies or wagons or some kind of furniture for the parlor—coat racks, maybe, or horsehair sofas— and not people at all.

I watched the other orphans peering intently into strange faces, trying to decide who might be good to them and who wouldn't. The little boys and girls did as they had been coached, pulling on coattails and asking softly, "Can I go with you and be your little boy?"

Was there maybe someone here, young and sweet looking, I could count on not to treat me un- kindly? I could go up to them and ask . . . but I was too embarrassed to do that. What if I pulled on the coattails of a person who didn't want a Polish girl in her father's boots? And what if she walked away and everyone could see I was unwanted? Why, that would be terrible. But likely there was no such person here anyway, so it didn't matter.

The farmers checked us over to see if our legs were strong and backs straight. One of them felt Spud's muscles, then stuck his dirty old hand in Joe's mouth to examine his teeth. Joe bit him, of course. Miss Doctor grabbed Joe by the arm and sat him in a far corner. I could not hear what she said to him, but her mouth moved faster than the wheels of the train. When she came back, she sent Sammy over to sit with Joe. No one would be taking those two particular orphans.

A friendly-looking man and woman stopped in front of Mickey Dooley, smile on his face and cap on his head as always. "How are you, young fellow?" the man asked.

"Fit as a fiddle, sir," said Mickey, his voice a little squeaky.

"Are you Irish?" the man asked.

"Yessir, indeed, sir," said Mickey Dooley, tipping his cap, his eyes looking this way and that at the same time. The man took the woman's arm and they moved on.

One farmer said Mickey was too small and his skin too fair for farm work, and a woman blessed herself when she saw his eyes. Mickey saw me watching. "There's a henway on your neck," he said.

"What's a henway?" I asked, feeling my neck.

"Oh, about six pounds," he said with a wink. Nothing made him unhappy, even being unwanted.

I could see lots of people stopping to talk to Lacey, she was so pretty and sweet looking. But the first thing she said each time was, "My name is

Lacey and I'm slow." And the people moved on.

"Lacey, over here," I called to her, as softly as I could to avoid being noticed. She climbed down off her end of the bench and came and stood in front of me. "Why are you telling people that?" I asked her.

"I want people to know about me straight out and choose me anyway."

I shook my head, knowing no one would choose her anyway. Maybe she was better off.

Two babies and three of the biggest boys were chosen first. Then Kitty, by a rancher and his wife with five little ones of their own. Children were being taken right and left. Some were crying at being separated from brother or sister, some laughing, some hanging on to someone else like they were straps in a streetcar and if they let go, they'd fall right down.

Poor orphans. What would happen to them?

A man and a woman dressed in shiny black stopped in front of me. They were tall and skinny as broomsticks with cold, squinty eyes and lips that looked like they hadn't smiled since Abraham Lincoln got his first long pants.

*Oh, no,* I said to myself, *I am not going anywhere with you. You look like you'd step on kittens.*

I stuck out my tongue, and off they swept, the Broomstick Twins, to give some other orphan nightmares.

A creaky old voice right beside me said loudly, "What about this one, Oleander? She looks capable enough."

"But she's so big and lumpy," said another voice. "And that nose. We could park our wagon in it. You think she might be Jewish, Peony?"

"Not with that yellow hair."

They were talking about me, those old ladies who wanted someone capable even if she had a big nose. They seemed cheery with their pink cheeks and bright eyes and flowers on their hats.

"We need an older girl," the person called Peony said to Mr. Szprot. "How old is this one?"

Mr. Szprot said, "Near fifteen, ma'am." I was hoping for lightning to strike him for that lie, but nothing happened. "She is very experienced with children."

"We got no children," said Oleander. "Just a mother and some old aunties. They need a lot of hefting and cleaning up after. Can she do that?"

"Can she lift a hundred-pound sack of flour?" asked Peony.

"And scrub a wood floor?" added Oleander.

"Is she sturdy enough of stomach to tend the chamber pots?"

"And wash old feet?"

"Can she sew, mend, launder, and iron?"

Mr. Szprot kept nodding, chewing his cigar, and saying, "Without a doubt, without a doubt," all the time looking at me with his beady eyes so I feared to say a word.

"Boil ashes and lye for soap? Butcher hogs? Hull, shell, grind, sift, boil, bake, pickle, and pop corn?" More nodding from Old Sourface.

"We'll take her," said Oleander and Peony together.

I knew it. Melvin was right. People didn't want children, they wanted feet washers and hog butchers.

"I don't want to go with these old ladies to be a nurse, a cook, and a slave," I said to Mr. Szprot. "How would it look if the Aid Societies placed me with them and I died of too much butchering and baking?"

Mr. Szprot chewed on his cigar. "We'll take that chance," he said.

"No, please, I don't want to go!" But Mr. Szprot was determined, and the frosty Miss Doctor wanted to get rid of all of us so she could read her book and brood. *I would rather die right here and now in some horrible fashion*, I thought, *than go with Peony and Oleander.* I would jump out a window. Or fling myself into a lake. Or throw myself in front of racing horses. But we were on the ground floor of a building miles from any water with lots of farmers and orphans but no racing horses. I was doomed to go on living.

While Oleander and Peony signed a paper for Mr. Szprot, Lacey came up and grabbed my hand. "I don't want you to go," she said. "I'm scared. I don't like to be scared."

"Quit hanging on me, Lacey. I have troubles of my own. And don't start crying." I wiped her nose on her skirt and pushed her back into line with the others. "It makes your eyes all red and your face snotty."

As we left, I saw Hermy the Knife being led by his ear by a big old farmer in overalls. I couldn't believe someone had taken Hermy rather than Mickey Dooley just because Mickey was small and pale and Irish and his eyes wandered. That was going to be one sorry farmer.

Peony and Oleander and I climbed into a wagon, and Oleander picked up the reins. If I didn't get out of this right now, I was doomed.

After a few minutes of clip-clopping, I said, "I don't want to go with you, you know."

"That ain't up to you," said Oleander. "We got this paper."

We rode a little farther. "I'm not as strong as I look."

"Doses of molasses and cod-liver oil will soon build you up."

More clip-clopping. "I can be difficult."

"We know how to handle difficult girls." She snapped her whip.

"Well, then," I said, "I will run away."

Peony and Oleander looked at each other and laughed. "Not much place to run to here on the prairie," said Peony.

Clip-clop, clip-clop, farther away from the train and closer to having to heft and sift and pickle for the rest of my life. *Mama? Papa? Help me. What should I do?*

*Use your head, Rodzina,* I told myself. *Mama and Papa aren't here but you are. Use your head.*

Clip-clop, clip-clop. I could barely see the lights of Grand Island behind us. Finally I said, "I'm surprised you wanted me, what with my being Polish and all."

"Don't know much about Polish," said Peony. "Ain't Jewish, is it?"

"No," I said.

"Polish ain't colored, is it?" asked Oleander.

"No," I said.

"Or Italian?"

"Or Spanish?"

"Or French? I won't have none of those heathens in my house."

"Oh, no. None of those."

"Polish is a good Christian thing to be?"

"Oh, yes. Why, we pray four hours every day. And do no work on Sundays. Or Wednesdays. Or Fridays. Or feast days. Or eves of feast days. Or . . ."

Oleander looked at me, slowing the horses down a bit.

"And we keep our bodies covered at all times. Never even take our clothes off to wash. We seldom wash. In fact, we *never* wash." Now Peony looked at me.

"And we fast by eating only meat. A lot of meat. Good beef and pork, bacon and lamb roasts. Why, we like meat so much, we even put ground earthworms in our bread. And I am very, utterly, earnestly Polish," I ended.

I watched to see how they had taken all this hogwash. The clip-clops got slower and slower and finally stopped. "Trouble," Oleander said.

"Big trouble," said Peony, looking me up and

down. Clip-clop, clip-clop again, faster and faster, as we turned in a big circle and headed right back to where we'd started.

I fairly danced out of the wagon.

The farmers and their wives had all gone home with the orphans they'd bought. Mr. Szprot and Miss Doctor stood outside, lining up the remaining children for a march back to the train. Peony found Mr. Szprot and tore up that paper right in front of him. They got back in the wagon and left with no orphan at all. I reckon just wasn't anybody good enough for them.

Mr. Szprot stared at me, his face like a thunderstorm brewing, so I lined up behind Miss Doctor with the rest of the unwanted children. Most of the big boys were gone. Horton was missing—taken, I guessed. But there were still a couple of the babies, including Nellie and Evelyn, with us, and I saw the rest of my group of unlovables: Lacey and Chester, Spud, Mickey Dooley, Joe, and Sammy.

"Rodzina," said Miss Doctor when she saw me, "Mr. Szprot said you had been taken. What are you doing back here?"

"They didn't seem to like Polish people," I said.

She frowned at me. "You cannot just walk away from arrangements we have made for you. You are not in charge. We know what's best for you and are responsible for your welfare. We . . ." *What about being responsible for Gertie? What about her welfare?* Miss Doctor went on and on. Finally we began the walk back to the train.

There were more empty seats than before, I realized as I took my seat and scratched my knees. Now what? Would I ride this train forever, just as I had feared? Would I be sold to some other stranger? Or would Miss Doctor finally agree to send me back to an orphanage?

I knew I needed to keep my wits about me, but for a moment I pretended that this train was headed east, not west, and that Mama and Papa would be waiting for me at the Chicago depot.

"You must be hungry after all that traveling," Papa would say, taking my hand. Mama would take my other hand, and we would walk together to Auntie Manya's for pickle soup and sour rye. I would tell them about Mickey Dooley and jelly sandwiches and old Peony and Oleander, and we would laugh, being careful to be quiet so we didn't wake the boys.

Then I cried myself to sleep so quietly that no one could hear. Not even me.

# ☙ 5 ☙

# WESTERN NEBRASKA

"GO BACK TO YOUR seat, Rodzina," Miss Doctor said without even opening her eyes as I slid onto the seat next to her.

"I want to go back to the orphanage."

"I told you, orphanages are not equipped to keep children permanently."

"I will not go somewhere to be a slave. I'd rather die."

Miss Doctor opened her eyes. "The people who come for you orphans do not want slaves."

"No one takes orphans just to be kind. They want unpaid servants. Those old ladies—"

"They would have given you a home, Rodzina," she said, her *Z* buzzing like an entire hive of angry bees.

"They would have worked me to death and not mourned at all."

"Well, then, Miss Brodski, tell me exactly what it is you want, and the entire mechanism of the Association of Aid Societies, the great city of Chicago, and the sovereign state of Illinois will not rest until they find you exactly the right home."

I figured she was making fun but thought I'd tell her anyway. "Maybe a nice family who wants a daughter, not a servant. With a mama and a papa and some little kids. Boys maybe. Little boys. And I would like them to have a house and a yard and plenty to eat."

She rolled her eyes. "Anything else?"

"Well, they don't have to be Polish. Mama would like it if they were Catholic but Papa didn't think much of any religion at all, so I guess it doesn't matter. He said the Brodskis have been nonbelievers since the sixteenth century, when Pint-Pot Latuski became Bishop of Posen for a bribe of 12,000 ducats, and he did not plan to be the first to defect."

"You can omit the commentary, Rodzina." Miss Doctor took off her glasses and rubbed her eyes. "You are an orphan. If a family offers you a home, you will take it."

"*If* I will not be a servant. *If* I will be safe and warm and fed."

"We will do our best. We always do."

"You mean Peony and Oleander were your best?"

"Go back to your seat, Rodzina."

All night and the next day we rattled and swayed, stopped and started again. My body ached like I had spent the night toting rocks instead of just trying to sleep. Who would have thought someone could get so tired and sore just from rattling and swaying?

Out the window, the empty plains went on and on. Here and there were mileage signs for pokey little towns with western-sounding names: Dead Mule Junction 10 miles, Wild Horse Ridge 25 miles, Lick Skillet this way, Buck Snort that way.

When the train stopped in a town called Rotten Luck, Mr. Szprot took us out to stretch our legs. The air smelled of dust and cows. I watched the little kids carefully to make sure they didn't take off, get run over by a cow, or blow away in the dusty wind.

"My daddy could have named this place," said Spud.

"How do you mean?" asked Sammy.

"He worked at the lumber mill, saved his money, and bought a little store. Then he sold the store and bought a saloon. Then he began to drink, went broke, and went back to work at the lumber mill. Then he died."

"When my dad was drinking, he would whup me with the fry pan, to save me from the gallows, he said," said Joe.

"My pa used to whip me on the soles of my feet so no one could see," Chester added.

They all looked at me. "My papa never whipped me," I said.

"I'll tell you what I think about that in two words: im-possible," said Chester.

"Telling falsehoods is plumb wicked," sang Mickey Dooley. "Lying is a sin. When you go to Heaven, they won't let you in."

"Never," I said. And it was no lie. My papa was big, with big, strong hands. He always said Brodskis work with their heads, not their hands, but it was his hands that kept us alive. He went to the stockyards every day but Sunday, where he slit the throats of pigs born to be hams, lard, and leather for the people of America. Papa stood ankle-deep in blood as the squealing pigs came by, hanging from their feet by an overhead belt, and he took his strong knife and opened their throats. His feet swelled and blistered from all those hours on the hard floor. In the summer he tied a handkerchief over his mouth and nose to keep out the flies and mosquitoes, and the sweat poured off him. In winter the unheated room was thick with steam from hot water and hot blood, and he could barely see to cut the pig and not his own arm. In all seasons he came home stinking of pigs and fear. But for all his size and big hands, my papa was a gentle man. . . .

"Watch the rest of the kids for me for a minute," I said to Spud as I climbed back onto the train.

"Miss Doctor?" I said, standing next to her seat.

She opened her eyes and sighed.

"And they can't hit."

She closed her eyes again.

The next morning, while Mr. Szprot, cigar in his teeth as always, slept and Miss Doctor read her book, I sat and watched Nebraska go by. Slowly I became aware of a ruckus. The boys had plopped down in the aisle and were taking off their shoes and socks. "Goldurn," said Chester, looking at Sammy's right foot, black and crusty with grime, "I bet that's the dirtiest foot on this train!"

"Bet it ain't," said Sammy. Bet—the magic word.

Half the carload of orphans came over to look at Sammy's foot and their own, argue, and wager.

Then Sammy took off his other shoe and stuck his *left* foot into the air. He was right. *That* one was the dirtiest foot on the train. Peach pits and marbles went into the pocket of Sammy's patched knickers.

Then they all began to unravel their socks. I sure couldn't figure what they were up to. Whistling through a gap in his teeth, Chester wrapped the yarn around a dried-up old apple. He kept winding and winding, and after long minutes he had a ball.

What is it about boys and balls? If there is snow or a stone or an apple and some socks, there is a ball. And if there is a ball, there is a game. I know this because of my brothers, Toddy and Jan, who turned everything round or almost round into a ball.

One time when Mama was to be out late, she gave me ten cents to buy chopped meat so I could have dinner ready when she and Papa got home. While I was slicing bread, Toddy grabbed the meat, rolled it into a round shape, and threw it to Jan. Back and forth went the meatball until Jan made a wild throw, and it hit the ceiling and stuck.

"Get it down," I hollered, punching Jan on his arm, "or you will be the one to tell Papa his supper is on the ceiling."

Toddy lifted Jan, but he couldn't reach it. I lifted Jan, but he still couldn't reach. Toddy took hold of the packing crate that we used for a table and moved it over. I stood on it and lifted Jan, who was then able to scoop the meat off the ceiling. But my foot went through the crate and we tumbled to the floor, meatball rolling into a corner.

Toddy and Jan tried to fix the crate while I dusted off the meatball and turned it into meatloaf. Papa said it was the best he ever ate.

My remembering was interrupted by a plop on my head.

"Sorry, Potato Nose," said Chester as he retrieved the ball. Seemed Sammy, Joe, Chester, Spud, and Mickey Dooley had started a baseball game in the aisle.

Muffled shouts and cheers filled the car: "Yer out!"

"Not by a mile!"

"Slide, Kelly, slide."

"He ain't King Kelly. I am."

"No, me."

"I'm Cap Anson, star of the greatest team in the league, the Chicago White Stockings," said Joe.

"I want to be the striker," Sammy shouted.

"You?" said Mickey Dooley. "You couldn't hit a bull's butt with a bass fiddle!"

Sammy just laughed—Sammy, who swung at Joe every chance he got. But he didn't get mad at Mickey Dooley. No one got mad at Mickey Dooley. How could you get mad at a kid who was smiling all the time?

Lacey stood quietly and watched them. Then she asked, "What are you doing?"

"We're playing baseball, dummy," said Spud.

"What's baseball?"

"Why, only the greatest game in the world. Yer out!" he shouted at Sammy, loud enough to make Lacey jump.

"How do you play?"

"Git away, Cabbage Head. I got a game to play and you're in my way." Spud turned back to Sammy. "You're out, you no-good, cheatin' lowlife!"

"Ro, you tell me. How do you play baseball?"

Never having seen an actual baseball game, I wasn't at all sure, but I thought I could figure it out. After watching for a few minutes, I told her: "Okay, see, the thrower puts spit on the ball and throws it at the striker—that's the guy with the water dipper."

"Why?" she asked. "Is he trying to hit him?"

"Yes, but the striker tries not to get hit—because of the spit all over the ball, I'd say."

"Why is the striker waving the water dipper around?"

"He's trying to keep that spitty ball away from him. If he by chance hits the ball with the dipper, he runs and tries to hide. And if that guy over there catches it, why, they commence arguing about it."

"Run home!" Chester shouted to Joe. "Go on home!" How could they go home, I wondered, when they were orphans, or as good as, just like the rest of us? Home. I was too sad to talk to Lacey anymore, so I just shut down the explaining machine.

The baseball game turned into a boxing match. Chester sat on Spud, and Mickey cheered him on: "Smack him one! Hit 'im in the head. You can't hurt him there."

Spud and Chester went tumbling down the aisle, rolling like a bowling ball straight into Mr. Szprot. That woke him up, got Miss Doctor's attention, and put an end to the game in a hurry.

"SIT!" Mr. Szprot bellowed. "I don't want to hear a sound above a whisper from you louts. Sit there and thank God that you are here and not sleeping on the streets of Chicago."

At first there was silence, and then Mickey

Dooley said quietly, "As the mother skunk said to the little skunk, 'Let us spray.'"

They all erupted into laughter, and I thought Mr. Szprot might put us off the train right there in Louse Creek, Nebraska, but Miss Doctor pushed him aside. "Rodzina," she said, "take this rowdy bunch and keep them quiet."

"But Miss Doctor, I didn—"

"Rodzina!"

I decided to tell them a story. That always quieted my brothers. Toddy and Jan were not twins but were born so close together and looked so much alike, everyone thought they were, for you couldn't tell where Toddy left off and Jan began. When they grew from babyhood to little boyhood, they did everything together. They even died together in a fire, which devoured Auntie Manya's house while she was looking after them there one night. After that, Auntie Manya went away, and we didn't see her again, tiny Auntie Manya who smelled of mothballs and tomato soup. I had told Toddy and Jan stories each night, and after they died I just continued, even though they were not around to hear. For a long time in the dark I told stories to little boys who were not there.

The orphans all gathered in the front of the car,

close to the warmth of the stove. I settled myself in my seat by the window. Poking at some new holes in the knees of my stockings, I began. "I'll tell you about the time my papa won a pig in a raffle. He thought he'd lead it home on a string like a dog, but the pig, being no dog, just grunted and sat down. Papa tried to carry it. The pig squealed and squirmed so much, Papa dropped it and had to chase after it through the muddy streets until he caught it again. Papa decided he and the pig would take a streetcar."

"Get outa here," said Sammy. "You can't take a pig on a streetcar."

"I know that and my papa knew that, so he went into a bakery and got a flour sack. He put the pig in the sack, tied it up tight with string, and waited for a trolley. He paid his nickel, sat down, and shoved the pig underneath his seat. The pig began to squeal, and to cover the noise, Papa began to sing."

"What did he sing?" Lacey asked.

"That doesn't really matter. He—"

"But I want to know. What did he sing?"

"For Heaven's sake! Maybe 'Silver Threads Among the Gold' and 'The Song of the Polish Legion.' Now can I continue?"

Lacey smiled and nodded.

"Finally the pig grew silent."

"Was he dead?" asked Lacey.

"No, he was just quiet. Unlike you. Papa sat back and relaxed. And then an awful smell filled the streetcar. The air grew greenish and thick. The smell was coming from where Papa was sitting. People stared at him. They grumbled and moved away. Finally the streetcar rumbled to a stop, and the driver stood up and looked at Papa. Papa looked at the bag and the dark stain slowly spreading on it. He stood up, picked up the bag of pig and pig . . . stuff, tipped his hat, and got off the streetcar." The orphans at my feet began laughing and slapping their knees—quietly, so as not to arouse Mr. Szprot again.

I finished my story. "He walked all the way home with that sack stinking in the sunshine. Even on Honore Street we could smell him coming. We ate on that pig for a month and laughed every time."

"I never heard of a sack full of pig before," said Mickey Dooley, "but I once knew a man had a sack full of snew."

"What's snew?" Lacey asked.

"Nothing. What's new with you?"

That Mickey Dooley. You never could get anything out of him but a joke. He was happy as a fly in a pie. He could be mighty annoying with his jokes, but I thought he must be the happiest kid I ever saw.

Everyone started telling funny stories then about their folks. "My pa," said Spud, "was so lazy, he used to hire someone to do his snoring!"

Sammy said, "We was so poor, even the cockroaches were starving."

"My ma was the knittingest woman you ever saw," Mickey Dooley put in. "She'd take yarn to bed with her at night, and every once in a while she'd throw out a sock."

And another day passed on the train, taking me from a lonely Chicago to who-knows-where. I ate jelly sandwiches, washed faces, stopped fights, and told stories.

Toward suppertime all was quiet and I had a few minutes to myself. I watched out the window. Soon we would be in Cheyenne, and someone else might want to take me, and I would not want to go. What would happen to me? Through the growing dusk, I could see distant tepees, herds of grazing animals, dark unknown shapes. My thoughts were as gloomy as the night.

The train stopped at an eating station but, occupied with our cold potatoes and wrinkled apples, we did not get off. The water tower, painted with an advertisement for Stonebreaker's Indian Gum Syrup for the Gut, was ringed by emigrant wagons. As I watched, families tended horses, pitched tents, and unloaded big iron kettles, rocking chairs, and old battered trunks tied with rope.

I imagined Mama and Papa there with them, going west. "My Rodzina," Papa would say, "my little jelly doughnut. Come down from that train and join us in our wagon. We will all go west together and open a restaurant, where we will sell your mama's egg noodles and poppyseed cake."

"Polish girl," Mr. Szprot called to me from the door of our car. "Come here."

What now? I got up and plodded over to him. "I do have a name," I told him.

"What?" Mr. Szprot asked.

"Me. I have a name. Rodzina. My name is Rodzina."

He and Miss Doctor stepped off the train and motioned me to follow.

Mr. Szprot said, "Polish gi—" but Miss Doctor interrupted. "Miss Brodski," she said, "we must send some telegrams from the station here. We want you to keep the children quiet and orderly."

"Make everyone stay put," Mr. Szprot added.

I nodded and climbed back on the train. I was completely in charge. My chest swelled with importance.

"All right, you guttersnipes," I said to the orphans under my command. "Pipe down and stay put."

The car was full of giggles and snorts. I gave them the stink face. "What's so funny?" Not a word. I looked around. "Where's Lacey?" The whole car exploded into laughter.

Spud pointed out the window at the covered wagons. "I told that copperknob those was circus wagons," he said through his guffaws, "and there was clowns and acrobats and an elephant. And the dummy believed me!"

"WHERE IS SHE?" I bellowed.

"Out there," he said, "going to the circus."

Radishes! I wasn't even in charge for five minutes and one of the orphans was missing!

"I'll go get her. All of you stay here!" The girl *was* feebleminded. A circus indeed! I tore out the back door and over to the wagons.

It was a mild evening for early April, not quite dark yet. Folks were sitting around a fire, and there was Lacey in the middle, eating cornbread, with butter and a big smile all over her face.

"Lacey," I called. "Come here." The folks all turned to look at me.

"You the body told this child we was a circus?" one woman asked.

"No, that was Spud. He enjoys tormenting Lacey because she is slow. Come on, Lacey. We got to get back before Miss Doctor and the Szprot do."

"Now, wait a minute," said a gent with long skinny arms and big yellow teeth like piano keys. "You don't want to let that Spud fella think he got the best of Little Miss here." He scratched his sunburned nose. "Have a seat. We ain't no circus, but I can do this—" He pulled six potatoes out of a sack and juggled them like a regular music-hall fellow. I knew we should hurry back, but I had never seen someone juggle potatoes before, so I sat.

"And I this." An old man pulled out a fiddle and began to play "Turkey in the Straw," while a black-and-white dog walked on his hind legs, an old lady in a yellow sunbonnet pulled an onion out of Lacey's ear, and a fat little boy did ten somersaults in a row. Lacey and I ate pie and popcorn and drank apple cider, so good after our days of jelly sandwiches, and we clapped and cheered.

I was worried about getting back to the train, so after ten minutes or so we wrapped the rest of the popcorn in a newspaper cone, said hasty goodbyes, and hurried off.

Miss Doctor and Mr. Szprot were already on the train. The car was hectic and noisy. I heard Mr. Szprot say, "Where in tarnation is that Polish girl?"

"I'm here, I'm here," I said as we clambered up the steps. "Just stepped out for a breath of air."

I passed by the boys in their seats and gave them an if-you-say-anything-I'll-clobber-you look.

"You, Polish girl," said Mr. Szprot, grabbing my arm and twisting me around, "are useless. You will be leaving us at the next stop; I don't care if you're taken by grizzly bears or men from the moon. You are gone!"

Tarnation! He might as well throw me off the train right here to be picked up by whatever wretch-on-horseback happened along. My stomach wobbled. I could have used some of Stonebreaker's Indian Gum Syrup for the Gut right about then.

Once the train started up, the boys came over, giggling and poking at Lacey. "Did ya see the circus, Lacey?" Spud asked. "Were there animals and clowns and acrobats?"

Lacey's eyes shone in the reflected gaslight. "Oh, yes. And a magician and a dancing dog. It was wonderful. I never thought to see such a thing as a circus." She unwrapped the newspaper bundle of popcorn, put a few kernels in her mouth, chewed, and swallowed. "But I wish we could have stayed to see the elephant."

The boys all turned toward me. "What is she talking about?" asked Spud. "That was no circus."

I smiled sweetly. "I think I liked the juggler the best," I said as I settled down next to Lacey. "And the pie."

At that the boys all ran to the end of the train and, pushing and shoving each other for a better view, looked out as we pulled away, leaving the wagons far behind.

The train rushed through the night. After a long time a warm red star twinkled near the tracks, and we came upon a tiny wayside station with gray windows and people waiting outside. Some people got off the train. Where were they going? What did they want? What were they looking for? In a flash the train was off again and they were left behind. All was darkness again. Did those people have any notion how almighty lonely they were going to be?

## ❧ 6 ❧

# CHEYENNE

NEXT MORNING I BUMPED into Mickey Dooley at the water bucket. "Know what kind of fish live in a water bucket?" he asked, his eyes as usual looking here and there at the same time. He didn't wait for an answer but waved the dipper at me and said, "Wet fish. Get it? Wet fish."

I wanted to keep on thinking my dreary thoughts and not be interrupted with fish jokes. "Why do you keep joking about nothing all the time?" I asked him. "We're coming up to Cheyenne, where we'll be sold like chicken feed to farmers. Aren't you worried?"

"Water you mean?" he asked.

"Why—" I began, and then stopped my questions. His left eye had managed to quit its wandering and look right at me. I could see sadness there. Why, I reckoned he was just as worried as I was. He just couldn't say so. I figured the least I could do was pretend right along with him. "Wet fish! You sure are one funny fellow, Mickey Dooley," I said as I took the dipper he handed me. "Wet fish."

Back at my seat I watched out the window again. The flat, stubbly prairie looked like Papa's face when he needed a shave. Here and there were herds of animals Chester thought were antelope. Or moose. Or elk. Sure weren't buffalo, he said.

Luncheon? Apples and jelly sandwiches, of course, but by now the bread was dry except where the jelly had soaked in and made it soggy, and the jelly was mostly crusty sugar crystals, which crunched between my teeth. We also had milk and hard-boiled eggs that Szprot had bought at our last stop, but my mouth longed for something sour—a dill pickle or sauerkraut or Mama's headcheese with vinegar.

Nellie came and leaned against my legs. "I don't want to go west," she said. "Spud said the west is full of murderers and guns and wildfires. I'm plumb scared of the west." She was little and pale, and I was still worried that Miss Doctor would get rid of her, like she did Gertie, so I put aside my own thoughts for a moment.

"No. He's wrong. West is a good place to go," I told her. I lifted her up and settled her between Lacey and me. "My mama used to tell me a story about the west, when we first came from Poland, heading west to a whole new country. Seems there was a—"

"Once upon a time," said Nellie, nose dripping on my sleeve. "That's how stories start."

"Okay, then. Once upon a time in a town far away in Poland lived a tailor named Matuschanski. He was a very tall man with a very long nose and a very long beard. And he was so thin, he could pass through the eye of his own needle, so thin he fell through the cracks in the sidewalk, so thin he could eat only noodles, one at a time. But he was a kind man and a very good tailor."

Lacey snuggled closer to Nellie so that she could listen, until all three of us were pressed right up against the window of the train.

I went on. "One day a Gypsy passing through town cut her foot on a stone. She came to see the tailor, who darned it so neatly there was no scar. As payment, she read his fortune in his palm: 'If you leave this town on a Sunday,' she said, 'and walk always westward, you will reach a place where you will be king.'"

Chester and Mickey Dooley came and sat on the floor by my feet. "'Well,' said the tailor, 'I will never know whether or not she was right unless I go.' And so Pan Matuschanski packed up a bundle with a needle, a thousand miles of thread, and a pair of scissors."

"A thousand miles of thread?" asked Chester. "Im-possible."

"Possible in this story. Just listen. All the tailor knew of west is that it was where the sun set, and so he walked that way. After seven days he reached the kingdom of Splatt.

"Now Splatt had troubles. The king had died, and it was raining. It was pouring. Everywhere else it was sunny, but over Splatt it was raining and had been ever since the king died.

"The townspeople moaned, 'Oh, who will stop the rain? It comes in our windows and chimneys, floods our roads, washes away our flowers, drowns our fish.'"

"Drowned fish!" Spud and Joe, who had joined the bunch at my feet, laughed so hard at that they fell over in a heap, kicking and punching each other. Sammy jumped up and separated the two, made Joe sit down next to him, and motioned for me to go on. I never before saw Sammy *stop* anyone from fighting. A small miracle.

"The princess of Splatt said, 'I promise my hand in marriage to the person who can stop the rain.'

"The tailor liked the idea of marrying a princess and becoming king. He thought and thought. Hmm. Rain. From the sky. Ever since the king died. Hmm. 'I know!' he shouted finally. 'Your king was so great and mighty that when he died and went to Heaven, he made a great and mighty hole in the sky. It will rain forever unless that hole is sewn up.'"

"Never happen," said Spud, who was sitting next to Lacey now.

"Happened here," I said. "So Pan Matuschanski had the townspeople take all the ladders in town, tie them together, and lean them against the sky. Then he took his needle and his thousand miles of thread and climbed up and up and up. When he got to the sky, sure enough, there was a huge hole in it. He went to work and sewed and sewed. Two days later, fingers stiff and back sore, he climbed down the ladder.

"The sun was shining in Splatt. 'Long live the

king,' said the mayor, handing him a golden crown while the townsfolk all cheered.

"'And,' said the princess, handing him a jeweled scepter, 'long live my husband.' And he did."

When I finished, Nellie was asleep against my shoulder. Lacey was sleeping too. And Mickey Dooley, Spud, Chester, and Joe. "May we all be kings in the west," I said with a great sigh, as I leaned back in my seat. "Or at least safe and happy." And I slept too.

When I awoke, the other children had scattered back to their own seats. Suppertime and Cheyenne, the last stop for the orphan train, drew near. We stopped in the middle of nowhere for a few minutes. Out the window I could read wooden grave markers lining the road: "Called Home August 12, 1880," one said. And "Ma Dyed 7 October 1869." And "Lillian Bruxton, mother of 12, grandmother of 32, greatly loved and greatly missed, dwelling now with God." The ground was littered with iron stoves, sofas and chairs, tables, and wagon wheels. What awful thing had happened here?

I walked back to the lady doctor's seat. She was smoothing her skirt and examining little holes made by the blowing sparks and cinders.

"Miss Doctor?" I asked. She picked up her

book from the seat beside her, and I sat down. "Why is all this stuff out here?"

"The railroad tracks appear to follow a wagon road," she said. "I imagine that as the road gets harder, people lighten their loads. And the markers note the resting places of those too old or too sick or too tired to travel anymore."

Why, can you imagine those poor souls throwing Mama's piano out the back of the wagon because it was too heavy? Or burying a grandma in the dry, hard ground, marked only with an old buckboard seat, and leaving her behind? It made me so awfully sad, my eyes burned for that imaginary grandma buried out here in the middle of nowhere.

Between these sad reminders were hundreds of tiny mounds like fairy hills. Plump little animals, looking like fat-cheeked squirrels with no tails, bounced and scolded as the train started up again. "Prairie dogs," said Miss Doctor.

Watching them took my mind off the world's sadness for a time.

Their furry bodies popped in and out of doorways in those mounds like they were passages to some underground world. I could imagine tunnels under the land leading to prairie dog cities, prairie dog rivers and lakes, prairie dog castles with a prairie dog princess with jewels in her hair and tiny pink slippers on her furry feet. When I started thinking about her prairie dog mama and papa, I could see this imagining was leading me somewhere I didn't want to go, so I took a deep breath and sat up straight. All the tears still uncried inside me, I figured, would make an underground lake at least as deep as anything those old prairie dogs ever saw.

"Miss Doctor?" I asked again, looking over at her.

"Here," she said, handing me her book. "You might find that this answers your questions." *Where to Emigrate and Why*, it was called. Miss Doctor was heading west to live, just like us orphans, just like those people in the covered wagons, just like the Polish tailor. Seems like everybody thought west was a good place to go. I wondered just why she was going. Had she really answered an ad for a wife, like I imagined in Grand Island? Or would she sew up a hole in the sky and marry a prince?

I knew Miss Doctor would likely not answer *those* questions, so I turned to the book to see what it could tell me. Cheyenne, the book said, was named for the Cheyenne Indians, who used to live and hunt all through these plains, but of whom there were not many left because the white folks, after calling their town after them, killed them. Magic City of the Plains, some folks called it, but more often, according to the book, the town was called Hell on Wheels, on account of its being lawless and rough. In fact, it was said, only one man had ever died there with his boots *off* since the town began.

We pulled into the station just at suppertime. The vast sky was growing dark, but I could see tepees, cabins, tents, and a few wooden houses strung along the bank of a creek. A muddy street led to the hotel. By the looks of the rest of the town, folk must have been awful proud of that hotel, it having three whole stories. Cheyenne sure was no Chicago. Guess it took only a handful of houses, a brick church or two, and a lot of saloons to make a city in Wyoming Territory.

The Western Hotel, Saloon, and Billiard Parlor sagged a bit, but there were red plush sofas in a lobby that smelled of floor wax and cigars. On one wall were hung the stuffed heads of poor dead animals, their glass eyes staring straight at me. It was almost enough to put me right off my supper.

Fortunately there were no dead heads in the

dining room. Folks had set out a covered-dish supper, mighty welcome after jelly sandwiches. Some of the people of Cheyenne appeared to be bankers or farmers or ranchers, but most were dressed in leather and fringe, looking like they'd just come in from the wilderness. I fully expected Dan'l Boone to walk up and ask to take someone home.

We orphans circled the tables where food was set out: platters of meat, bowls of turnips and potatoes, cakes and pies and hot, steamy cornbread. There were plates and forks but no chairs. I guessed we were expected to stand around and eat. And I was right.

Ladies in long dresses and aprons dished the food out onto our plates. I ate until I thought I'd bust right out of my dress. Afterward a pudding-faced lady in a hat with dead birds on it sang "The Last Rose of Summer." The winners of the school spelling bee spelled their prize words for us: *forlorn, impoverished, destitute, uncertain, outcast.* Those are the ones I remember, most likely because such things were heavy on my mind.

Some big bug in a black suit made a speech. I didn't listen, as I was occupied examining the room. These folks seemed friendly enough. Maybe Miss Doctor was right and not everyone was looking for a slave to wash the dishes or hoe the cornfield. Maybe there would be a family with father, mother, and kids, just some folk with a house to share, who wanted another child, not a hog butcher. Maybe . . .

When the picking and choosing of orphans began, Mickey Dooley got taken right away, by a youngish man and woman who looked nice enough to want a son and not a servant, but awful gloomy and sad of heart. I thought Mickey Dooley was just the boy to put a twinkle in their eyes and a dance in their steps.

"They look like fine folks," I said to him as they passed by.

"They promised me a room full of snew," Mickey whispered.

"What's snew?" I asked him as a goodbye present.

"I got me a family," he said. "What's new with you?" He winked at me and went off wearing a big smile and his new father's cowboy hat. I was sorry to see him go. All his jokes and cheeriness got on my nerves sometimes, but still it had been nice to know where I could find a smile if I needed one.

Evelyn and several of the babies were taken next. Nellie went with a gray-haired man and woman who looked like they wanted her very much and would never give her up. She gave me a tiny wave and a watery smile as she walked out with them.

A spindly-looking farmer and his wife took both Chester and Spud. Their new papa puffed out his chest with pride, as if those boys were just born to him right there that minute.

Lacey was standing next to me. "Now, remember, don't go telling people you're slow," I said to her, wiping a spot of applesauce off her chin. "You'll never find a proper home if you tell people right out like that before they get to know you."

"I told you, I don't want them to find out later and then not like me. Or send me back. I want them to know right off," she said. She turned and pulled on a woman's red wool sleeve. "Hello, lady," she said. "My name is Lacey, and I'm slow. Can I go home with you and be your little girl?"

The woman jerked away, looking at Lacey as if the girl had bird droppings on her head. "Will someone get this half-wit out of here?" she said. "No one will take her and she is making the others look bad."

I walked right up to the lady with my fists clenched. Lacey might be slow and a pest, but no stranger was going to call her names in my pres-

ence, no matter if she had brought gold and diamonds and fresh oranges in her covered dish.
"Lacey may be a bit slow," I said to her, "but she
is bright enough to know that it is rude to call people names. Unlike some others I see before me."

Miss Doctor marched toward me. It appeared I
was in deep trouble. But it was the woman she
grabbed by the arm and hustled away, saying,
"Rodzina may be too plainspoken, but on the
whole I agree with her. Let me show you to the
door. We have no child for you." Well, I thought,
maybe that lady doctor had a bit of a heart under
those clothes we were not allowed to touch.

She returned with a bald, bony old man trailing
about a hundred kids dressed in clothes much too
big, too small, or just too darned ugly. "Here is the
young lady I mentioned," she said to him.

"She good with young'uns?" asked the father.

Miss Doctor nodded. "She does what she is told
well enough."

The man walked around all sides of me, looking
me up and down. He stuck his hand out for me to
shake. "The name's Clench," he said. "Myrna's
the wife—she's at home watchin' over the place—
and this here is Weasel. And Lennard. Emmett.
Myra Jane. Purly. Sarah Dew. Lily. Buck. Fred.

Loretta. Big Bob. Concertina. And Grace." The children pulled at my hands and skirt, all talking at the same time, except for the biggest boy, who just hung back and glared. He had a pinched, unfriendly face, big ears, and a mouth overcrowded with long brown teeth. He looked to me like he should be Weasel, but seems he was Lennard.

"We need a right hearty girl to help with the young'uns," Mr. Clench continued, "and be another daughter to Myrna and me. And you'll do. Yessir, you'll do fine." It was done.

I felt like a sack of potatoes, weighed and measured and purchased. But he had said he wanted a daughter. Maybe this would work out.

While Mr. Clench signed a paper, I turned to Miss Doctor. "A family, with a mother and father and children," she said. "Give them a chance." She patted me awkwardly on my arm.

I nodded. "Find a good place for Lacey too, will you?" I asked her.

"We'll be here until Wednesday," she said. "Plenty of time to get all you children settled."

Mr. Szprot himself walked me to their wagon and helped Mr. Clench hoist me and my suitcase in among the bags of beans and flour. The children all piled in after, and off we went.

I was squeezed against the front of the wagon, boxed in by Clench food, Clench backs, and big, dirty Clench feet. At first I tried to keep as far away as possible, but as the night grew colder, I welcomed the warmth of even these skinny bodies. We plodded on mile after mile in that wagon behind a poor mule who looked like he needed a ride more than we did. The farther we got from the lights of Cheyenne, the stranger I felt. Where on earth were we headed? What would happen to me there?

"How far is it to this homestead of yours?" I asked Myra Jane, who seemed near my age, maybe a little younger.

"Near twenty-five miles. It's too blamed far to come to town regular, so we jest come twice a year for flour, beans, salt, tobacco, and such. And you." She smiled. "Sure are glad to have you. We don't ordinarily see no other folk but two, three times a year, being our nearest neighbor is six miles away. And he's too ornery for visitin'."

"Six miles!" I said. "What about school? Where do you all go to school?"

"We don—" Sarah Dew started, but Mr. Clench turned around and pinched my cheek. "You just settle back and sleep. We'll be home by morning."

I leaned my head against a flour sack but could not rest. In the sky shone an evil gray moon. My thoughts were all tumbling around. Morning? Too many kids? No neighbors. No school. What a pickle I was in!

We rode on and on, the wind whipping dirt into my eyes and that's why I might have looked a little weepy. But I wasn't crying. No siree. I had got what I asked for. Why would I cry?

## ❧ 7 ❧

# THE PRAIRIE
# EAST OF CHEYENNE

A PALE SUN WAS STRUGGLING to shine when I next opened my eyes. We were riding through a bleak and windswept landscape. Not a building, not a house, not a person, not a tree. My whole body ached from sleeping in a wagon, and I was hungry. Still, part of me hoped that maybe this would turn out well, and that in a warm house somewhere breakfast was waiting for us.

When we pulled onto a small rise in the flat sameness and stopped, Myra Jane shouted, "We're home!"

I looked around. Sarah Dew laughed. "You're lookin' for the house, right? Why, it's here underneath us." She jumped down and threw open a door in the dirt heap. "This is our dugout. We built it ourselves. Ain't it grand?"

"What on earth is a dugout?" I wondered aloud. What it was was a cellar or cave dug into the little hill. But for the door and the stovepipe sticking up, you couldn't tell that house from any other bump in the prairie.

We all climbed out of the wagon, some faster than others and me the slowest of all. A couple of mud brick steps led down into one small room, dirt floored and dirt walled. More dirt fell from the ceiling, which was, of course, also dirt.

The dugout was cold and dark as midnight. Mr. Clench lit a lard lamp like the one we had at home, and I felt a feeling like a sock in the stomach. Home. What if Mama was waiting for me in here? And Papa? And they said, "Rodzina, at last you have come." And Mama would give me a glass of tea with sugar and honey cake for breakfast.

I shook my head and looked around the dugout. In the dim light I could see a saggy bed in one corner, a wooden-box table with a nail keg for a chair in the other, and a little potbellied woodstove in the middle. It looked—and smelled—like animals might live there: bears, maybe, or prairie dogs. But certainly not people, not like this, in a hole in the ground.

The Clench children were bouncing around, looking at this and touching that, like they were happy to be home. A sudden, furious coughing made us all turn—bumping and jostling each other, it was that crowded—toward the bed in the corner. There lay a woman with her hair all stringy and a thin, sad face. Her bony hands kept moving in a fidgety sort of way. "This here's Myrna Clench," Mr. Clench said to me, his words making little puffs of steam in the cold air. "She's ailin' a mite."

"Hello, ma'am," I said with a sort of curtsy that felt like the right thing to do, but I did not go too near her for it sounded to me as if what was ailing her was not a mite, but mighty bad indeed.

Mr. Clench pushed me closer to the bed. "This is Rodzina, Myrna, come to live with us." He pinched my cheek again, turned me around to show her all sides. "She's a sturdy thing, ain't she?" he said.

I stood there shivering, with my shoulders hunched against the cold, rubbing my hands together to warm them. Here I was, off the train, with a mama and papa and some kids and a house, and it was all wrong. I didn't want to be here. I wanted to go home. To Honore Street.

While the wind roared outside, we huddled together to breakfast on cold beans and what Myra Jane said was hoecake but tasted to me like last week's sweepings. The Clenches all gobbled like pigs and chickens, smacking their lips and fighting for more. I had to push and shove like the others to get my share.

Afterward, Myra Jane shooed the boys out and gathered the younger kids around the stove. "Where's your outhouse?" I asked her.

"Pa says the whole world's our outhouse and no one has a prettier. But Sarah Dew and I dug a trench out back for ourselves. You can use that if you shovel a little dirt in afterward. Just watch for the boys. They're out lookin' for greasewood and buffalo chips for the fire."

Greasewood I could figure out. But buffalo chips?

"Dried dung," said Myra Jane when I asked.

I shuddered. Those hoecakes were cooked over dried *dung?* What kind of place had I landed? In Chicago we didn't have much, but we had coal picked from the railroad yards and broken grocery boxes for fuel. Newspapers sometimes. And we had a real wooden outhouse out back with a door and a roof.

After employing the trench and the shovel, I stood on that prairie, all wind and cold and loneliness. My hair blew into tangles and my nose ran, but at least here outside the dugout there was space and fresh air and nobody dying.

When I returned, Myra Jane showed me how to twist hay and weeds into tight little bundles for the stove, in case the boys didn't have much luck finding buffalo chips. They spent an awful lot of their lives finding fuel and building up a fire to try to keep warm, I thought. And it was April. What would it be like here in January? I shivered just thinking of it.

"Where's your pa?" I asked Myra Jane. I hadn't seen him since we first arrived.

"Huntin'. Fishin'. Or diggin'. He ain't here much. We purty much do what gotta be done." Seemed Myra Jane, Sarah Dew, Lily, and Loretta did the washing and mending and cooking and planted a bit of a garden in the summer. Concertina, now she was three, looked after little Grace. The boys patched cracks in the dugout, searched for fuel, and did some fishing when the rivers were running. They all took turns killing and skinning rabbits and hauling water from the creek two miles away. "And Lennard is a bone pilgrim."

"A what?"

"Bone pilgrim. Don't you know anything? He walks the prairie lookin' for bits of buffalo and cow bones. Sells 'em when we get to town."

"What on earth do folks want with bits of bones?"

"Make 'em into buttons and fertilizer and collar stays, Lennard says. We don't care long as he gets cash money for beans, Pa's tobacco, and suchlike."

Mrs. Clench commenced coughing again. "Myra Jane, Sarah Dew, Lennard, anyone," she called in a weak little voice. No one paid her any mind at all. She called again.

I stood up and said, "Guess *I'm* going to have to tend your mama," but that didn't shame any of them into doing it, so finally I went over to her.

"I need to use the thundermug," she said to me, "but it's too full."

Thundermug? What in blazes was a thundermug? She motioned toward a rusty old coffee can that apparently served as a chamber pot. I didn't mind too much emptying it. I had done such chores for Mama when she was sick. I took the can outside and threw the contents into the trench—

after first checking the wind to make sure none of it would fly back onto me. I rinsed it with a little water from the rain barrel, took it back inside, and helped Mrs. Clench to use it. Then I straightened her bed as much as I could. Her sheet and blanket were threadbare and filthy, swarming with bedbugs big as summer plums. I sort of smoothed her hair back and tied it with a piece of string I pulled from the blanket. She thanked me over and over. "My own kids don't care a bean for me," she said. She didn't sound sad, like you'd think she would. She just said it as a matter of fact, like "Sure is cold in winter." That was the saddest part.

"Where you from, girl?" she asked me.

I told her some about Chicago, and Mama and Papa dying, and the orphan train.

"Your family wasn't sickly, was they?"

"No, just unlucky, I think."

"That's fine. You as strong as you look?"

"Guess so."

"Good teeth?"

"Good enough to eat with." I was puzzled by her questions.

"Fine, fine," she said, and she closed her eyes.

"You kids should take care of your mama," I said to them as I joined the twisting again.

"Don't do no good," said Myra Jane. "You give her water or fix her blankets or clean her up, and afore you know it, she wants you to do it again."

"But she needs your help. And she's your mama."

"Not for long. Pa says she's apt to up and die on us anytime now."

I couldn't believe my ears. "Don't you care? My mama's dead, and I'd give anything to have her back." Once after Mama died, I found a discarded hunk of bread in the gutter and stuffed it into my mouth like a hungry dog. *What would Mama say if she saw me*, I wondered. Then all my sorrow and loss and longing hit me and I lay down and cried right there on the icy Chicago street and people had to walk around me to get where they were going. Yes, I'd have given anything to have my mama back.

Myra Jane poked me. "I asked, what did she die of?"

"Did she die of the galloping consumption like our mama is?" Sarah Dew asked.

"No. It was something else," I told them. The day Mr. Wcydozky told us Papa was dead at the stockyards, kicked in the head by a runaway horse crazy from the smell and sound of pigs, that was when Mama started dying. She got weaker and weaker, so when the fever came, it carried her right off. "I nursed her as best I could, brought her water, brushed her hair, and washed her face. You can do the same for your mama." I thought of all the orphans who'd pay their last nickel—if they had a nickel—to have a mama, ailing or not. My eyes watered and I wiped them on my dress, but I swear it was just the smoke.

"Pa says not to fuss—he'll jist get us a new mama," said Sarah Dew.

"But you're a family. You got to take care of each other."

Suddenly Myra Jane leaped up, grabbed a shotgun off the wall, and aimed it right at me. *Psiakrew! I shouldn't have preached at them*, I thought. *Now Myra Jane's mad as blazes. She's going to shoot me, and I will die an orphan!*

She swung the barrel a bit to the right before pulling the trigger. The gun was almost as loud as my heartbeat. Dirt sprayed everywhere. "Are you a crazy person," I shouted at her, "shooting that gun in here?"

She said nothing but bent down and picked up a snake, yellow with dangerous-looking orange stripes.

"Myra Jane," I said, "you saved my life." I hate snakes worse than the Kaiser, the Devil, and Otto Bismarck, as Papa used to say.

"This ain't nothing but a hungry old rat snake lookin' for the mice that nest in the roof," she said. "It wouldn't hurt nobody. And it ain't bad eatin'."

Eating? Not me. No sir. In my life I had eaten pigs' feet and duck's blood and cow's stomach, but I wasn't eating any snake. No sir.

Sarah Dew brought in a kettle full of water from the rain barrel. Myra Jane put in some greens, a few withered potatoes, and the chopped-up snake. "Stew," she said to me with a smile.

"What else you eat around here?" I asked her, hoping for something besides snake stew and hoecakes.

"Mostly jackrabbit, prairie dog, catfish, sage hen—whatever Pa and the boys find out there. In the spring we grow a few greens and things before it gets so hot that everything dries up and blows away. In the fall there's wild plums, fox grapes, and ground cherries. And we most always got beans."

Me, I'd starve to death out here. Who could live on snakes and prairie dogs? No roast pork with prunes? No sauerkraut? No spice cake or fresh lemonade or stuffed cabbage rolls? My stomach growled, and I sighed.

Mr. Clench came home around suppertime. "Smells mighty good," he said. "I can always trust my girls to make me a supper fit for a king." He licked his lips and gave me a big smile as he sat down on the nail keg by the table. Sarah Dew gave him a bowl of stew, and I ladled out a cupful for Mrs. Clench. The rest of them stood around the pot and shared out the stew with one spoon. The first few times the spoon came to me, I shook my head, but finally I got so hungry from the smell and all the hay twisting and mama tending I had done, I took the spoon and had me a heaping spoonful of snake stew. It was hot and didn't taste too bad. Not *kiełbasa* or roast pork but a sight better than dried-up old jelly sandwiches. There was silence in the dugout until every drop was gone.

After her cup of stew cooled enough, I fed some to Mrs. Clench, spoon by spoon. She didn't want to eat, kept shaking her head and turning away, so I distracted her mind by telling her about the orphan train and Miss Doctor.

"A lady doctor?" she asked. "Are you sure?"

"I'm sure. Of course right now she's just a nursemaid to a trainful of orphans, and she doesn't seem to think much of the job."

"A lady doctor. Imagine." Mrs. Clench swallowed some stew and shook her head. "Me, I wanted to be a schoolteacher. Thought I'd like that, all dressed up in starched cottons, pointing at a map and saying, 'Now what is the name of this state here east of Wyoming?'"

"Why didn't you?"

"Married Clench at fourteen, had all these here babies, and soon I'll be dead as a beaver hat. That's my whole story."

"Your mama and papa let you get married at *fourteen?*"

"My mama was dead and my papa was drunk and no one asked if I wanted to." She looked at me. "How old are you? You look to be fifteen or so."

"Twelve," I answered. "And I don't want to get married. Or be a schoolteacher or a lady doctor." I was thinking so much about me at that point that I entirely forgot to spoon stew into Mrs. Clench. "I want to go to school and come home and do homework on the kitchen table and talk about all the things that happened that day. I want someone to tell me when to go to bed and boil eggs for me at Easter." I swallowed hard. "Guess what I want is my mama and papa back."

Mrs. Clench leaned back on her pillow and waved me away. "I'm plumb tired out from all this eating and talking," she said.

I helped Sarah Dew and Myra Jane scrape off the dishes, spoons, and pot. "Myra Jane, if you show me where the broom is, I will sweep up a bit," I said.

Myra Jane snorted. "What hay and dry grass we got, we burn. Ain't none to waste on frippery like brooms. You better learn that right off." Perhaps this was for the best, for I had no idea how to clean that place when I couldn't tell just where the dirt ended and the house began.

Lennard banked the fire, and the others pulled horse blankets and quilts out of a wooden trunk. We girls wrapped ourselves in the blankets and settled on the floor—all except for Concertina and Grace, who slept in the bed with Mr. and Mrs. Clench.

The boys went outside. "They sleep in the wagon," Myra Jane said.

"Ain't it awful cold out there?" I asked her.

"They come in if it starts snowin'. They ain't stupid."

Lennard stepped on me on his way out. "Why does he hate me?" I asked.

"He don't hate you. He hates ever'one," said the girl to my right. Lily? Loretta?

"Why?"

I could feel her shrug. "Way God made 'im, I reckon."

Sarah Dew snuggled up on my left side. "I want to sleep right close by you. I won't get to when you move to the bed."

Why, I wondered, would I get to sleep in the bed? Maybe the children all took turns. I thought of the bedbugs and shivered. I preferred the floor.

It was as noisy in the dugout that night as if the whole city of Chicago was sharing it with me instead of just one family. The wind screeched and whined, Mrs. Clench coughed, Mr. Clench snored. The girls were restless, twitching and murmuring and snorting.

When I finally fell asleep, I was as restless as the rest. My dreams were part memories, part nightmares. I was walking down the stairs from our house on Honore Street. Mr. Czolgowicz, the super, grabbed my arm and said, "You need a place to sleep, *kopytka*. I got a bed. Are you willing to share it?"

I ran from him. The night was growing darker and colder. Delicious smells came through the open door of a tavern near Canal Street, and I stopped to sniff. "Pretty lady," whispered one man loitering outside the tavern, "come home with me and I will feed you roasts and chocolate cakes." Another grabbed my arm and shouted, "Wrap those long legs around mine, dearie, and I will buy you beer." And he turned into Mr. Clench.

I was wide awake now. I feared I was in a fix. I lay there scared and worried all night and never did go back to sleep.

The next day it rained. Mr. Clench hung around the dugout, watching me and getting in everyone's way. I ignored him best I could. I took care of Mrs. Clench and cleaned her chamber pot again. I showed Myra Jane and Sarah Dew how to mix up some cough syrup for her from onions and sugar, the way my mama showed me. "Didn't nobody ever teach you this?" I asked them.

"Papa said we should every once in a while tie a piece of peppered meat on Mama's chest, but we ain't often got meat to spare," Myra Jane answered. "And we won't have to worry about that when she's gone and you're our new mama."

A terrible fix!

I took to hiding behind Clench's children as much as I could, to keep away from him. I changed Grace's diaper, told stories to Lily and Loretta, and helped Myra Jane cook up a pot of beans. Big Bob took to me like ants to a picnic. Every chance he got, he climbed on my lap, stuck his thumb in his mouth, and went right to sleep. Because of my brothers, I've always been partial to little boys, their dirty little hands and the sweaty smell of their hair. I sat a long while with Big Bob in my lap and smelled his hair.

Right before supper Clench grabbed me. "Let's go for a little walk, you and me," he said. I gave him the stink face, but he just laughed and pinched my cheek. "Now, none of that ornery stuff. You better learn to like me. You're gonna be here a long time."

"Leave me alone!" I shouted. "I'm too young for this. I'm only twelve!" Clench laughed again and hugged me. "Don't touch me! Go away!" The children stood around us, looking mighty pleased at the thought of a new mama.

Who was there to help me way out here? *Mama! Help me, Mama!*

"Elgin, leave that child alone!" I thought for a minute Mama had actually heard me and was coming from Heaven to help. "You ain't gonna ruin another girl's life like you ruined mine." It was Mrs. Clench, who had pulled herself to her feet. "Why, she ain't hardly older than your own daughters. Take her back to town and find yourself someone who is old enough and willing to be a mama to my children, or I swear I will haunt you from the grave."

Mr. Clench let go of me. I think like the rest of us he was shocked to see Mrs. Clench standing up and not just lying there like she was dead already. He stalked outside and never came back all that night. I sat on the bed, huddled against Mrs. Clench, until morning, when Clench came stomping in. "Git your suitcase and git in the wagon," he said to me. "I don't want to waste any more time on this trip than I have to."

Was he really going to take me back? I looked at Mrs. Clench. She nodded. "Go on," she said, "and find someone to boil Easter eggs for you."

I grabbed my suitcase and climbed up out of the dugout and into the wagon. We started off. The last I saw of the Clench youngsters, they were sitting in that poor patch of dirt they called a garden, breaking up dirt clods with sticks, knives, and their bare hands. Big Bob was crying. Only Sarah Dew waved goodbye.

The whole way back to Cheyenne I sat stiff, my suitcase on my lap, ready to jump down and run if Mr. Clench seemed liable to grab me again. He didn't. He didn't look at me and he didn't say a word. That was just fine with me. I kept searching the distance, straining to see the first lights of Cheyenne shine out across that lonely prairie.

By nightfall I was again at the hotel. The desk clerk took me into the parlor, where Miss Doctor was drinking a cup of tea and Mr. Szprot a beer, just as we orphans had suspected.

"He didn't want a daughter," I told Miss Doctor, who shielded me from the Szprot's fury. "He just wants a new wife for when the old one goes."

"I'm sure you're mistaken," she said to me as she led me from the parlor and up the stairs. "Certainly he could see you're much too young to be someone's wife."

I looked her in the eyes but said nothing for long minutes. Finally her face grew red. Maybe she was beginning to believe me. "The old coot," she said. "I'm sorry we got you into that. I never thought that . . . Well, I never thought. He'll never get his hands on another orphan, I promise you." I nodded at her to let her know she was forgiven and that I trusted her to keep her promise. "Now get into bed with Lacey. We will figure out what to do with you tomorrow."

It was my first night ever in a hotel. The mattress was thin and lumpy, but the room didn't rattle-rattle-rattle all night, no one snorted or snored, I wasn't going to be anyone's new mama, and the bedbugs were just regular size.

Lacey pressed herself up against my side. I could see her smile in the moonlight. "I was lonesome when you went," she said. "I don't like to be lonesome."

"Seems to me there's a mighty lot of things you don't like," I said. "You don't like to be lonesome; you don't like to be scared. What *do* you like to be?"

She thought for a minute, her face all scrunched up, and then she smiled even bigger. "Full of pie," she said.

# ❧ 8 ❧

# WYOMING TERRITORY

WE SAT IN THE WAITING ROOM at the depot, kicking our feet against our suitcases while Miss Doctor and Mr. Szprot sent and received telegrams. Once in a while I scratched my knees. Nobody said anything. The unclaimed orphans—Sammy, Joe, Lacey, and I—were being sent back to Chicago, to a workhouse, where we would work for our keep. Mr. Szprot was grumbling about having to take us all the long way back to Chicago. Sammy, Joe, and Lacey weren't any too happy about it either. Me, I didn't think a workhouse sounded very good, but no worse than being sold to some farmer. Or married to Mr. Clench. I was feeling awfully low. Was there no place for me, safe and a bit cheery, with a family who wanted a daughter and had plenty to eat?

I wondered how the rest of us were, those orphans who had been taken by families. Were they merely servants washing dirty laundry and digging in the fields? Or were some of them happy with their new families? Did they have soft beds and porch swings and kisses good night? I hoped Nellie did. And Chester, Spud, and Mickey Dooley. I missed Mickey Dooley. I could have used a joke right about then.

We sat kicking our suitcases until Miss Doctor and the Szprot came over leading a big fellow, wide as a door, in overalls and leather boots the color of dried blood. "This gentleman," said Mr. Szprot, "has agreed to take our Sammy and give him a good home. Come forward, fortunate boy."

Sammy jumped up and tried to run, but the fellow grabbed him and smacked him on the head. Sammy skidded across the floor, right into the woodstove. We all jumped to our feet, but no one said a word. There was an awful silence, like the whole world was waiting to see what would happen next.

Mr. Szprot chewed on his cigar a time or two, then hauled off and punched the man so hard in the nose I thought his overalls would fly off. The big man hit the ground. "These kids is in my charge," Szprot said. "*I* smack them when they need smacking." Then he grabbed the leather boots and dragged the man outside, without disturbing his cigar one whit. He dusted off his hands, pointed to us, and said "Sit!" You can bet we sat.

Szprot and Miss Doctor went back into the telegraph office, where they shouted at each other, waving their arms around furiously as if shooing invisible pigeons away. Finally we saw him tip his hat to her and leave the depot.

We waited a long while. I got tired of kicking my suitcase and got up to read the notices posted on the walls:

## J. White and Company.
27 Prairie Street. Photographs 25 cents.
New methods. No holding long poses.
This establishment has the best
arranged light in the Territory.
Up one flight of stairs only.

## Know Thyself!
Heathcliff M. Piddleman,
Professor of Phrenology,
will examine the 37 organs of your brain
and indicate your character and talent.
RECEIVE A WRITTEN RECORD OF YOUR EXAM.

THE LATEST AND MOST SUCCESSFUL
REMEDY FOR CONSUMPTION, COUGHS,
AND COLDS—WILBOR'S COMPOUND
OF COD-LIVER OIL AND LIME.

## THE WESTERN PALACE THEATER,
★ 8 PM this evening ★
the IRVING BRIGGS Company of Thespians
will perform a new play in two acts,
MAID OR WIFE?
OR, THE DECEIVER DECEIVED.
The principal characters will be played by
Mr. Briggs, Mr. Loblolly, Miss Hartley,
and Miss Copeland. Overture Composed
and Conducted by Mr. Briggs.

The morning was nearly gone when Miss Doctor came back. "I telegraphed a friend of mine from Chicago who now lives in Ogden, Utah Territory," she said, "where she and her husband run a hotel. And I have received her answer. She thinks some folks there would be willing to take in orphans. So you will not be going back to Chicago. We will go on to Utah." Joe and Sammy and Lacey gave a big cheer, but I was too worried about who would want me and for what. "You must behave yourselves and be agreeable and not trouble me. Do you understand?"

We all nodded. "Can we say goodbye to Mr. Szprot?" I asked her. I never liked the old sourface much, and he sure didn't seem to like me, but he had been with us since Chicago, and he had stood up for Sammy when it counted. I thought he deserved at least a goodbye. But Miss Doctor said he was already on his way back to Chicago for another bunch of orphans.

"Here," she said, handing us some bread and apples, "go and eat while we wait for the train."

Although it was bitter cold outside, the sun was shining. I could see what looked like storm clouds in the distance. "Is there a thunderstorm out there?" I asked a man loitering on the platform.

He looked to where I pointed. "Why, missy, those are mountains. The Rocky Mountains."

I could not imagine hills stretching so far into the sky, farther even than the grain elevators on Chicago's River Street. But it didn't surprise me. I had seen so many strange things on this trip across this big country that very little would surprise me anymore.

"Those clouds are the Rocky Mountains," I told Sammy and Joe and Lacey when I joined them.

Sammy had taken off his cap. He wiped his head with his handkerchief, spread the handkerchief on his lap, and put his bread and apple there.

"Watch out!" shouted Joe, but too late. A rat near the size of an alley cat ran up and grabbed Sammy's cap. Well, Sammy took out after that rat while we all laughed like to fall right off the platform. The rat ran north and south, Sammy ran north and south, the rat ran back and forth, Sammy ran back and forth. Finally the rat dropped the cap off the end of the platform into the dirty snow. While Sammy climbed down to get it, the rat doubled back, picked the hunk of bread off Sammy's handkerchief, and ran the other way.

Why, that rat knew just what he wanted and figured out how to get it. I found myself admiring him, and things got to be real bad for a body to admire a rat.

Finally we stopped laughing, and Sammy stopped fuming and sputtering. Lacey shared her bread with him and we all ate.

"That rat sure outsmarted dumb old Sammy," Joe said. "But I won't tell no one. It'll be my secret."

Sammy frowned at him. "You ain't one that ought to make jokes about secrets."

Joe jumped up, his hands balled into fists.

"I think animals *are* smarter than people sometimes," I said, anxious to avoid another fight. "Papa told me about a mule at the stockyards. That mule knew exactly how many wagon loads he should pull from the killing shed to the yard in one day, and when that number was pulled, be it noon or nine, he would pull no more. And never would he pull a load on a Sunday."

Sammy nodded. "Lions in Africa attack only men, never women and children."

"That ain't so," said Joe.

"It is."

"How do you know?"

"Just know, that's all."

"Birds who live on the side of a hill lay square eggs so they don't roll away," I said.

"That sounds like hogwash to me," said Sammy.

I looked up from my apple and saw, on the far end of the platform, my first Indians. Such a sight to remember and tell to . . . well, I had no one to tell, but it was a sight anyway. Real Indians, in faded pants and blankets, calico skirts, some with beads and feathers in their hair. For sure I wasn't in Chicago anymore.

Slowly the station grew crowded. High-booted,

shaggy-haired men in overcoats made of woolen blankets or wagon rugs, wrapped around with ammunition belts, washed themselves under the pump. Faded, worn, anxious women bounced chubby children in their arms. There were men in spectacles, women with lunch baskets, pretty girls and wailing babies.

"Lookit all them guns," said Joe. He was right. Seemed like everyone but the babies had guns.

"That's because of Big Nose George," Sammy said.

"Who's he?" Lacey asked.

"You don't know about Big Nose George? Why, he's the most fearsome train bandit riding the rails today. Robbed some four hundred trains and got away each time. Killed three men in Texas for looking at his nose. Threw an old lady off a train in—"

Lacey started to cry. "Oh, rubbish," I said. "It's only a story of Sammy's. If Big Nose George were real, I would have seen a wanted poster for him, familiar as I am with the notices hung in train stations, and I have not."

Lacey looked up at me and smiled. Her tears flashed on her face like diamonds. What a face she had. No one would ever call her Big Nose Lacey or Potato Nose or some other ugly name.

I put my hand over my own nose, walked to the edge of the platform, and stared at the empty tracks pointing west toward the mountains. Behind me I could hear the moaning of the train whistle. I turned toward the sound. A little black dot grew bigger and bigger as the clanging and tooting got louder and louder until, with a burst of sound and steam like a hot Chicago summer, the train pulled in.

We boarded with everyone else and found seats in what Miss Doctor said was a third-class car. It seemed first-class to me—few orphans to tend, no jelly sandwiches, no Szprot.

Sammy and Joe sat together. I sat behind them with Lacey. And behind us Miss Doctor took a seat next to a lady in a red coat and a hat with cherries on it.

The seats were only hard wooden benches, but Miss Doctor got us each a straw cushion for sitting and sleeping on. They were two dollars each. Doctors, even lady doctors, must make a powerful lot of money, I thought.

The Indians did not enter the cars but stood on the landings between them. Maybe they liked the fresh air and didn't mind the almighty cold and wind. Whatever the reason, I was just as glad not to be too close. I didn't know what Indians were likely to do. I kept my stink face on awhile, just in case.

As the train started, Lacey jumped and ran up the aisle as if her feet were on fire. She scooped up a fat gray cat and carried it back to our seat, where they snuggled together like potatoes and gravy. The conductor, coming by to check our tickets, said with a wink that the cat was employed by the railroad. "To keep down the mice," he said.

"Does she have a name?" Lacey asked.

"Just cat, I reckon," the conductor answered her. "And she's a he."

"Well, he's got to have a name. Ro, what should his name be?"

"Let's see, he's so round and plump and soft," I said, "I think you should call him Dumpling."

"What's dumpling?"

"A dumpling is a fat ball of dough boiled and served with Mama's pork roast and sauerkraut," I said. "A dumpling is the best thing in the world."

"Then he is Dumpling," Lacey said.

I looked around the car at all the people going west. Or wester, since it seemed to me we were already in the west here in Wyoming Territory. What were they looking for? And why did they think it was way out here?

I turned around to ask Miss Doctor, but her eyes were closed. The lady sitting next to her was youngish and plumpish. Her face was as round and rosy as a china plate with flowers painted on it, and so jolly looking that I'd bet she smiled even while she slept. She was alone, but looked much too happy to be an orphan.

"Did you come all the way from Chicago like we did?" I asked her.

She shook her head no, and the cherries on her hat bobbled. "From Omaha. Going to be a mail-order bride." And she laughed a great, rumbly laugh.

"What is that? Can you order a bride from Mr. Montgomery Ward's catalogue like you do pianos and stew pots?"

She laughed again and said it was almost that easy. "I answered an advertisement in the Omaha *Herald* from a homesteader in this here Wasatch, Utah Territory, looking for a wife. We wrote a few letters back and forth, and here I am, going west." She smiled, and her eyes all but disappeared in the rosy folds of her face.

"I saw an ad like that in the Grand Island railroad station. A man in Montana wanted a wife. But aren't you worried about marrying a stranger?" I asked her. "Don't you mind leaving your home and family and all?"

"Got no family," she said. "And home was a room in a boarding house with mildew on the wallpaper and the stink of cabbage in the halls. Didn't aim to spend the rest of my life in that room or up to my elbows in scummy water washing linen for rich ladies who didn't want to wash their own. So when I saw that advertisement, it was like God said, 'Merlene, put down them buckets, dry your hands, and come out here to my country where the air is clean, the sky big and blue, and any dirty wash you do will be your own.'"

"What about him?"

"Who?"

"Him," I repeated. "You know. The man who placed the advertisement."

"Oh, *him*. Name of Enoch Thompson. He sounds kind and lonely. Not too young anymore, but neither am I. I foresee we'll get on well enough. I get on with most people."

"What if he doesn't want to marry you? What if he wants someone smaller or taller or older?" I was trying to understand this whole mail-order-bride business.

She snorted. "Men out there got to marry anything that gets off the train."

"What if *you* don't want to marry *him*? What if

he's mean? Or ugly? Or a criminal hiding out from the law?"

"Now, child, sometimes you got to trust and hope, not be saying 'what if' all the time. Besides, if we don't suit each other, I won't stay. I got my assets—hands and feet and a strong back. And at least I'll be out of that boarding house in Omaha."

Miss Merlene closed her eyes. While I watched her, I thought about this mail-order husband of hers. Would he be tall and handsome with a handlebar mustache and a horse and buggy, like the hero of a story? Could someone find all this out in advance so she would not be stuck with a Mr. Clench? Or did she have to hope and trust and not say "what if" all the time, just like Miss Merlene said?

Her eyes were still closed, but I asked her anyway, "Don't you mind that it's all so strange and unfamiliar here? People carry guns and live in dugouts and there are Indians on the landings."

"I like strange and unfamiliar," she said, opening her eyes just a slit. "It ain't the same old thing. And as for the Indians, poor souls, they ain't allowed to come inside, but they can ride for free out there. It's in the treaty. We get their land and they get the landings between railroad cars." She shook her head. "Wc white folk straight out robbed them, I reckon."

Miss Merlene went back to her nap then, and I turned to watch Wyoming Territory go by outside the window.

Lacey and the cat snuggled next to me. "Dumpling and I need a last name," she said. "You got a last name, and Mickey Dooley does. I reckon Sammy and Spud and Joe got last names, too. Everybody but us got two names. What could our last name be, Ro?"

"Well, pick a name. Any name. Like off that sign there," I said, as we passed a barn with a sign painted on.

"I can't read."

Sighing, I read it aloud: "Connery Grain and Manure."

"Manure," said Lacey. "It's pretty."

I sighed again. "Sure is, but I think Connery would go better with Lacey." So then she was Lacey Connery, and the cat was Dumpling Connery, and they both sat there and purred.

Snowflakes began to fall as the train climbed and turned. In some places we went so slow, it felt like they were laying track right in front of the train, so slow that what had been only blurs became bushes, scrub grass, and stunted pine trees poking up through the snow.

After a while we halted at Sherman and got off to stretch our legs. The sun was bright overhead, but still the air was bitter and sharp with the smell of cold earth. The conductor pointed out the sights, which weren't much. Sherman was a bleak and wild place, just a settlement of maybe a dozen houses, a little brick hotel, and a saloon set among low hills and snow-covered red rocks. A mighty wind stung my face as I read aloud the wooden sign posted there: "You are standing 8235 feet above sea level."

"Highest point on the route," said the conductor, pointing to the sign. "From here we'll go downhill fast as lightning through a gooseberry bush."

Lacey kicked at the ground a few times and buried her face in Dumpling's dusty fur. "What's wrong?" I asked her.

"This here highest peak. It's just more land. Why, I thought it would poke right through the clouds to Heaven."

"Ain't quite that high, Lacey," I said. I myself wished it was. Papa was in Heaven. "Welcome to Heaven," he'd say to me. "It is a wondrous beautiful place. Reminds me of Poland. Mama is here too, cooking roast goose and dumplings for you and God."

We walked around Sherman a bit, breathing the frigid air that burned my nose and chest and made my eyes water. There was a cliff with people's names carved in it. If Hermy the Knife was still here, I could borrow his knife and add my name: *Rodzina Clara Jadwiga Anastazya Brodski, an orphan going west, April 1881*. And it would be there forever and ever. I stood there at the highest point on the railroad line and looked east and west—saying goodbye and hello. The west sure was different from Chicago, and I didn't know if it would suit me.

I was already back in my seat when Miss Doctor boarded the train, followed by Lacey, Joe, Sammy, and the other passengers. She looked out of place in her black suit amidst all the horse-blanket coats and gingham dresses. And the black suit wasn't crisp and sharp anymore, marked as it was with red jelly and gray fuzz and what looked mighty like tobacco juice. I was surprised she hadn't changed into clean clothes.

Her face was so pale and unhappy that I found myself with a funny feeling. Pity. I pitied Miss Doctor. You got to be in a real bad fix to admire a rat *and* pity Miss Doctor.

She sat in the seat behind me. I turned. "Miss Doctor?"

She looked away from the window, her gray eyes more sad than sharp. "Miss Brodski?"

"Joe said Mr. Szprot said you're going to California. That true?"

"That's true."

"Well, what I want to know is why? You don't seem like the kind of person to want to go west. Aren't you a good enough doctor for Chicago?"

Her eyes sharpened right up at that. "I am a fine doctor, with excellent skills and training."

"Then why?"

"Because people in Chicago don't seem to take to a lady doctor, and I can't eat plans and dreams." She turned and looked again out the window. "I hoped it would be different in a new state like California."

"Miss Doctor?"

She made a little impatient motion with her hand, and I let her be.

After Sherman we raced back down onto flat plains and then, after the chimneys and fences of Laramie, started to climb again into hills of wind and desert. The earth was red and the land was lifeless, littered with dead trees, ox bones, and abandoned wagons. A shabby, hand-lettered sign read "New York City: a million miles away." I knew just how that fellow felt.

Here and there were lonely settlers' huts, which reminded me of the Clenches and my narrow escape. We stopped at stations with sad names like Bitter Creek and Point of Rocks. People got on and off, although I could not see where they were going to or coming from. The Indians at the front of our car left, and I breathed a breath of relief.

At the supper stop we ate in one of the eating stations I had so long admired from the outside. For three dollars all five of us ate meat soup, pie, sweet potatoes, pickles, raisins, bread, and coffee. The coffee reminded me of Papa's Sunday smell—a little bit coffee, some hair tonic, and the clean fragrance of a starched shirt, so different from his sour, sweaty everyday odor.

The land changed as we climbed again. There were rocks as big as buildings, and evergreen trees looking almost human as they waved their branches at us in the wind. Snow fell, the wind roared, and the train rattled and swayed west.

# 9

# A THOUSAND MILES
# FROM OMAHA

WASATCH STATION WAS our first stop in Utah Territory. Miss Merlene was the only passenger to get off the train. A man who had been leaning against the What Cheer Eating House walked over to her and tipped his hat. I wiped the steam from the window and pressed my nose against it, the better to see this mail-order husband of hers.

He was not what I had imagined, no fairy-tale hero at all, being a spindly fellow and a mite shorter than she, with a lot of grizzled gray in his beard. His coat sleeves didn't reach his wrists, his pants were so short I could see his stockings bagging around his skinny ankles, and he carried a fistful of weeds or sagebrush or maybe just the ugliest flowers I ever saw. But the moony way he looked at his bride and took her arm made my heart twirl around. It was as if she was a treasure made of glass or spun sugar, and he the lucky man who won her at the fair. If you asked me, they would hit it off just fine. Lucky Miss Merlene. I waved to her, but she never took her eyes off him long enough to see me. As they walked off, the cherries on her hat bobbled cheerfully.

"Echo Canyon," the conductor called, walking through the cars a while later, "now entering Echo Canyon." Enormous cliffs, red as the Polish flag, rose on both sides of the tracks. If I squinted my eyes, they looked almost like the brick mansions of the rich on Prairie Avenue.

"What is this word 'canyon'?" I asked him, for I had never heard it before.

"It's a Spanish word, missy. Means a deep ravine or narrow valley, like this here one we're riding in."

Spanish. How far away from Chicago I was, here where they said things in Spanish. I took to watching out the window behind us at the scenery we had already passed so I could remember where I came from. That girl was me, that girl back in the room on Honore Street. Here, who was I? Was I anybody? And what was to become of whoever I was?

I was still moody and broody when we stopped at the Thousand Mile Tree, marking that we had come a thousand miles from Omaha. A thousand miles. A thousand seemed like an awful lot of anything—a thousand potatoes, a thousand sausages, a thousand oranges or oilcans or orphans.

We all got out and looked at this big old pine tree on the bank of a stream. Although it was midday, it was cold, with a wind that nipped and bit at my face. I pulled my too-small coat tighter around me. At least I had a coat. Joe and Sammy wore only shirts and sweaters and knickers, and they stomped and pounded their arms trying to keep warm.

People were picking up twigs and stones—to remember the place by, I guessed—and some had newfangled box cameras that were supposed to make pictures, but I didn't think there was much worth remembering, just that old tree and red cliffs and silence. I stood there for a moment thinking about loneliness. *How quiet and deserted it must be here*, I thought, *when the train is gone and the only sounds are wind and water*. I wondered how that big old tree felt when the trains pulled out. Would it be happy to be left alone? Or would it droop with loneliness, remembering the folks who used to visit and daydreaming about those to come?

We climbed back on the train. Miss Doctor sat alone in the seat behind Lacey and me. She began her usual sighing and clucking over her skirt. "Miss Doctor," I asked her, turning around, "why don't you just put on another skirt instead of fussing about this one?"

She blew softly through her nose. "I would wear another skirt if I owned one, but this suit is my only suit."

Her only suit? No wonder she had been so careful of it. "I thought doctors were rich," I said.

"Some, perhaps. But I am a doctor without patients, without prospects, and far from rich."

"Miss Doctor, if you can't get rich, why are you a doctor anyway? There aren't too many lady doctors around."

"My father was a chemist," she said. "He used to let me help him in his laboratory, teach me things. After he died, my world shrank to my mother's world—music lessons, china painting, and visits from other women with nothing to do. I wanted more." She took her handkerchief from her sleeve and dabbed at her nose. "I wanted to *know* things. So I studied medicine. Now I want to *use* what I know."

"Don't you want to get married and have babies? Mrs. Bergman, who lived beneath us on Honore Street, used to say that women need—"

"What women need is more exercise, shorter skirts, and their own way once in a while." She closed her eyes.

The train lurched suddenly. We were riding on the very edge of a cliff, stone walls hundreds of feet high on the right and, on the left, the wild river far below, rushing and splashing over the rocks.

Joe and Sammy pressed their faces against the windows, gleefully shouting, "We're goin' over! We're goin' over!" and "That was a close call!" and "Look at that curve ahead. We'll never make it! We're goners for sure." Miss Doctor kept her eyes closed, while Lacey and I looked down at our laps.

"Spooky," said Joe, pointing out the window.

I looked. The huge rocks seemed like the turrets and spires of ruined castles, where wicked witches might live, or one-eyed monsters, or ghosts. "Yeah, spooky," I agreed.

"Let's tell ghost stories," said Sammy. He pulled his sweater up over his head and stumbled up and down the aisle. "Where is my head? Booo! Where is my head?"

"Don't be dumb," said Joe, kicking him in the shin.

"Joe, don't kick your brother," I said.

"Joe ain't my brother," said Sammy, kicking Joe back.

I grabbed them and pulled them onto the seat with Lacey and me before the other folks in the car wearied of the racket and rumpus of orphans and threw us out the window.

"Ro, you tell us one," Lacey said.

I shook my head. "I don't know any ghost stories. Mama didn't like them. She liked happy stories."

"Make one up, then."

"Well, I could try, I suppose. Okay . . . once there was a little boy. He—"

"What was his name?" Lacey asked.

"Frank. Let's say his name was Frank. He—"

"How old was he?"

"Gee whiz, Lacey. That stuff doesn't matter." She stuck out her lower lip and crossed her arms. "Ten, okay? Let's say he was ten."

She nodded and I continued. "One night, one very rainy night, when the wind blew hard and lightning flashed and thunder rumbled through the land . . ."

Lacey squealed and pulled her skirt over her head. Good. Maybe now she would let me get on with the story. This was fun, this making up a brand-new story. ". . . thunder rumbled through the land, his mama and papa called him down from his bedroom in the attic. 'Frank,' they said, 'we must go out for a while. There are ghosts and spooky things abroad tonight, so you'd best stay in your room and keep the door locked.'

"Frank begged to go along, but his papa said, 'No, no, you must stay here.' So Frank locked the door behind them and crept up to his room in the dusty, spidery attic, where he sat down on his bed, all shivery and trembly from fear."

"He had to sleep in a room all by himself?" Sammy asked. "No wonder he was so scared."

"Quiet, you mug," I said. "Suddenly from downstairs came loud oo-ey noises."

"What are oo-ey noises?" asked Joe.

"You know, sounds like 'ohhhh' and 'oooo' and 'eeee' and such. Frank's face grew pale as a pork chop. The moaning got louder and louder.

'Fraaaaa-nk,' the spooky thing moaned. 'Where is Fraaaaa-nk?'

"Frank could hear the thing walking around downstairs—*ka-thud, ka-thud*. And then those *ka-thud*s became louder and louder. The thing was coming up the stairs—"

"Wait a minute," said Joe. "I just remembered. The door to the house was locked. How did it get in?"

"Dummy," said Sammy. "Spooky things don't need no unlocked doors. Go on, Ro."

"The thing was coming up the stairs, making more oo-ey noises and calling, 'Where is Fraaaaa-nk?' Louder and louder, *ka-thud, ka-thud*, until the door swung open with a bang, and there was . . ." I looked wildly around the car for inspiration, for I had gotten so caught up in my own story that I had failed to think just what it was, creeping up those stairs. ". . . and there was a woodstove clomping in, *ka-thud, ka-thud*, coming closer and closer . . ."

"A *woodstove?*" asked Joe. "That's what was so scary? A *woodstove* stomping up the stairs?"

"You better stick with potatoes and forget about stories," Sammy said. The boys laughed so hard, they fell right off the seat and rolled around the aisle of the train until Miss Doctor grabbed each one by an ear and sat them down next to her.

"That was a mighty puny story to tell boys, Rodzina," said Lacey. "It didn't even scare *me*. Even I ain't afraid of a *woodstove*."

Here I was taking care of those kids like I was ordered to, and all they did was complain. First they begged me to tell a story and then they grumbled because they didn't like it. You'd think since we orphans were all in the same boat, we could at least be polite to each other, but they weren't acting very polite. They could hurt someone's feelings if they weren't careful.

Well, no matter. I was finished with them now. Let them tell each other stories and answer their own dumb questions and wash their own sticky faces.

I stood up. Sticky faces reminded me: I ought to go wash mine before we reached Ogden. The water in the bucket had a layer of ice over it. *I'll wash later*, I thought. *Like in July*. So I just smoothed my hair and straightened my dress and sat down again. Maybe there was such a thing as hot water and soap in Utah Territory. I hadn't washed more than my hands and face since the orphan home and was starting to smell a bit like old cheese.

We pulled into the depot. *Here we go again*, I thought. I felt like a ham in a butcher shop, all pink and juicy and waiting to be bought and paid for.

It looked mighty cold and snowy outside. Miss Doctor had us gather our suitcases and follow her to the door.

"Here, now, little lady," said the conductor to Lacey, who was hauling Dumpling as well as her suitcase. "We can't have you taking that cat away." He lifted it from her arms.

"No, give him back to me." She stretched her arm up, but the conductor lifted Dumpling out of her reach.

"We need this cat, missy," he said. "Why, without him, the mice would eat us up in no time."

Lacey turned to me, face all red and scrunched up like a raisin. "Please, Ro, Dumpling wants to be with me. Tell the man to give me my cat."

"Tell him yourself," I said, ignoring her sad face and her eyes swimming with tears. "I have more important things on my mind than you and that cat." Not only was I sore at her for siding with Joc and Sammy, here I was facing slavery again. I turned my back as Miss Doctor took her arm and steered her away from the cat and the conductor.

The station was lonely and silent. We climbed down onto the platform, where an icy blast of wind near to blew us right back to Wyoming Territory. The cold made my teeth hurt, and the snow was blinding, sharp and hard. It encased my whole face in an ice blanket, and I had to keep slapping it to bits in order to breathe.

Two people, bundled up like Christmas packages, hurried over. Miss Doctor shook their hands and turned to us. "This is my high school chum, Mrs. Rutherford Tuttle, and her husband." We shook their hands too, and stood there nodding at each other until I thought we'd turn into icicles right there on that platform in Ogden, Utah Territory.

Finally Mr. Tuttle said, "It's much too cold for conversation out here. Let's get you and your bags and—"

Suddenly there was a cry of "You'll never tell, ya stinkpot! I'll croak ya first!" from Joe.

Sammy jumped onto Joe's back, shouting, "Oh, yeah? Well, I'll clobber ya, clonk ya, slug, sock, and conk ya!" And then a great splintering noise as Joe and Sammy crashed through the railing and fell six feet onto the frozen ground below.

Miss Doctor and the Tuttles raced down to them,

clucking and fussing like barnyard hens. "They are fine," Miss Doctor called up. "They might have a few bruises but no broken bones." I myself thought that a pity, for broken bones might have slowed down the wrestling a bit.

Juggling all our suitcases, I went into the waiting room, where I was joined by Miss Doctor, the Tuttles, Sammy, and Joe. I stomped my feet, broke the ice over my face, and breathed in the slightly warmer air as Miss Doctor examined the boys more closely. "We need sal ammoniac and tincture of arnica for those black eyes, but will have to do without. I am surprised that you don't have more serious injuries, the way you—" She suddenly stopped talking and looked around. "Where's Lacey?"

Nowhere. Lacey was nowhere. We searched the waiting room and the platform, but she was not there. Mr. Tuttle flagged the train, which was preparing to pull out of the station. While Mrs. Tuttle stayed inside with Sammy and Joe and me, he and Miss Doctor helped the conductor search every car and the landings between. But no Lacey.

Could she have lit out on her own? The Tuttles piled us into their wagon and headed toward town. We saw nobody, and the snow kept falling harder.

# ❧ 10 ❧

# OGDEN, UTAH TERRITORY

THE TUTTLES' HOTEL was a big, drafty barn of a place. The parlor, warmed by a huge stone fireplace, was crowded with stuffed sofas and chairs but, thankfully, no animal heads. Through an archway was a big wooden desk and a small wooden bar; opposite, stairs climbed to the rooms above. I had already been in a hotel before, so I wasn't too impressed.

Mr. and Mrs. Tuttle unwrapped themselves and proved to be tall, pretty people. She had a hat made of feathers perched on her pompadour. He had a lot of frizzy brown hair and was kind enough to notice how scared I was about Lacey. Taking my arm, he said, "Don't worry. Big Earl's coming to lead the search. He knows this country as well as I know my dear Kathleen's face."

Big Earl? Turned out he was the sheriff, a Rocky Mountain of a man with a turned-up nose and tobacco stains in his yellow mustache. "Wahl, now," he said, walking around a bit before sitting down and scratching his big belly. "Wahl, now, let's think."

There was a long pause while he fingered his mustache. Radishes! Was there no way to make this sheriff fellow *move?*

"Wahl," he said again, "it's almighty cold outside. I'd say she musta headed for shelter. That's just common sense."

"Poor Lacey ain't got common sense," said Sammy, wiping his teary nose and eyes on his sleeve. "She's feebleminded."

I jumped up. "No, she ain't. She's just different. A mite slow."

"Don't matter anyhow," said the sheriff. "Don't mean she ain't got common sense. Why, even a goose got common sense, and geese is sure a far sight slower than any little girl." There was another long pause while the sheriff scratched his chest and snapped his suspenders. "Wahl, I'll go fetch Angus, and we can search to the west toward Merton's place. Tuttle, find Buster and head south.

There are a few homesteads that way. The boys," he said, nodding toward Joe and Sammy, "can do what Mrs. Tuttle needs doin' here. And you," he said to me, "keep this fire going strong. We're gonna need it by the time we get back."

As the men left, the sheriff patted Miss Doctor on the shoulder with a hand like a bear paw. "Don't you worry none, little lady. You just stay here and try not to worry. I'll find that youngster— got to, or the Boss will have my hide."

"Isn't *he* the boss?" I asked Mrs. Tuttle.

Mrs. Tuttle smiled. "He calls his mother the Boss because she's so much bigger than he is." Bigger than Big Earl? My eyes bugged. I would have given a hundred dollars, if I had a hundred dollars, to see *her*.

All afternoon Miss Doctor and I sat watching the blowing snow—me at the window to the left of the fireplace, Miss Doctor to the right. Each time the door opened, I jumped, but only the wind and a few strangers came in. No sheriff and no Lacey.

After too many hours of this, Miss Doctor came over and put her hand on my shoulder, but I shrugged it off. She left without saying anything. A short time later she was back again. "Talk to me.

I am worried about Lacey too, and I think we could ease each other."

"I want no ease from you," I said. "I want nothing from you but to be left alone." Suddenly all my bad feelings of the last few weeks bubbled over like sewage in Bubbly Creek near Honore Street. "How could you?" I shouted. "How *could* you let Lacey get lost? You were responsible for us, but you care for nothing but yourself and your books and your dumb old skirt!"

I stopped to catch my breath and wipe my eyes with my fists. "You don't care about us at all, and now Lacey is lost, and it's your fault!" I looked right at her.

"I am doing the best I can," she said, her cold voice surprisingly small. "I am a doctor, not a baby nurse. But I am doing the best I can." Her glasses fogged over so I could no longer see her eyes. She gave a jerky little wave and went back to her seat to the right of the fireplace.

"Well, your best is not good enough," I called after her, but not very loud. "In fact, your best is . . . lousy."

I fed wood to that fire until it was hot as Hades in there. I don't mean to curse; I mean Hell itself couldn't have been hotter than that parlor, but feeding the fire was something for me to do besides fret.

After a while I started to feel bad about what I'd said to Miss Doctor. And I wasn't sure Lacey's disappearance actually was her fault. I was afraid it might be mine.

Had Lacey run away because I had snapped at her? Did she go somewhere to cry at my meanness and lose her way? Did she kidnap Dumpling because I wouldn't help her find another way to keep him? I regretted how cruel I had been to her. No, not cruel. Just not real friendly, a bit cold and standoffish. Wrapped up in myself. Kind of like Miss Doctor. . . . I did not want to think about *that*. I threw a log the size of a locomotive on the fire.

Each day for three days the howling wind banged at the doors and rattled the windows as if trying to get in and warm itself by the fire. Each night for three nights the searchers came back shaking their heads. Miss Doctor and I didn't talk at all. She sat with a book in her lap but didn't read. I felt restless, just sitting and brooding and occasionally feeding the fire, so I took to walking up and down the hotel's two flights of stairs—up and down, up and down. Finally Mrs. Tuttle said, "Here, use up some of that energy mashing turnips and setting the table." So I did, but still I brooded.

Mrs. Tuttle cooked us hot soups and buffalo stews that Miss Doctor just picked at, but the worrieder I got, the more I ate. One night I dreamed of cabbage, and everyone knows that means bad news.

Finally, in the afternoon of the fourth day, Big Earl, followed by a crowd of searchers with red noses and frozen hair, came back with a small bundle in his arms. He laid Lacey down on the sofa and stood back. Miss Doctor hurried over to her, but I stayed where I was. There was dead silence. Dead. No. I couldn't stand for someone else to die. My hands were shaking.

"Found a barn, she did," the sheriff said. "She and that cat. Knew she had enough sense to find shelter." He didn't sound like he was about to tell us Lacey was dead. I stood up. "She was nestled in the hay with a cow and her calf. Pretty as a little red wagon in a wheat field."

He stroked her forehead, and she said loudly, "Put the milk in the meat grinder, Ro. Night is coming."

"She's alive," said the sheriff. "For now."

Everyone let their held breath go and rushed to

gather around the sofa, pointing and yelling: "Pack her in ice so she don't thaw out too fast."

"Rub her hard with a rough towel."

"Whiskey. She needs a slug of whiskey and so do I."

"NO!" Miss Doctor shouted. "Get away. Don't rub her. There might be some freezing there yet. No ice—she's cold enough as it is. And she doesn't need any whiskey, though I'd say you all could do with a drop."

Mr. Tuttle placed a smaller bundle on the floor before the fire. Dumpling, shaky and half frozen, but alive. He looked up, gave a weak meow, and commenced licking his tail. Dumpling, it appeared, was fine. Lacey, though, was in a bad way, shivering and babbling.

"Get a tub in here and fill it with warm water," Miss Doctor said, which Mrs. Tuttle and I did while Miss Doctor stripped Lacey's clothes off. We lowered her into the tub and watched as her white and pinched face and hands slowly began to turn pink again. Still she shivered and babbled.

Finally we lifted her from the tub and wrapped her in all the spare blankets we could find. Miss Doctor sat by the fire with Lacey in her lap the rest of the day, humming a soft little song. Frosty as the lady doctor was, I could see there was something straight about her. She probably *was* doing the best she could, just as she said.

I watched Miss Doctor and Lacey, continued to feed the fire, and drew trees and cats with my fingertip on the foggy windowpanes.

Around suppertime Mrs. Tuttle came in and put her hand on Miss Doctor's shoulder. "Come and have a bit of supper, dear," she said. "I will watch the little girl."

Miss Doctor shook her head. "No, I can't leave her. Not now."

"But—"

"Later, Kathleen. Not now."

Me, I went and ate supper. When I returned, Miss Doctor was still holding Lacey. I sat a minute and watched them. Miss Doctor was tired and pale, but her face, when she looked down at Lacey, was soft and almost gentle. I felt a twinge in my belly that I knew was not hunger, seeing that I had just eaten. "Miss Doctor," I said, my voice a little creaky from not being used all these days. "Miss Doctor, I want to apologize to you. I know Lacey getting lost wasn't all your fault, and I'm sure you do care about us in your own cold sort of way."

She looked up at me and whispered, "No, you were right."

I was shocked into silence.

"I should have taken better care of all of you," she continued, "instead of being so consumed by my own troubles. I shall try to do better."

I had a question I could not have asked the frosty Miss Doctor who did not care about orphans, but I thought I could ask this new soft and almost gentle Miss Doctor. "Seeing Lacey there in your lap reminds me. I want to know about Gertie. She whined and complained something awful, and she mussed up your only skirt, but did you really have to abandon her in Omaha?" Miss Doctor looked up but I went on. "Did you just leave her at the railway station or did you at least find her a place to sleep? And were there other—"

"Wait a moment. Do you mean the little green-eyed girl who left the train in Omaha?"

"Yes. That girl. Gertie. Did you—"

She looked at me quizzically. "You think I just dumped her off the train?"

I was about to tell her that yes, that's just what I thought, but she continued. "Gertie 'complained something awful' because her arms and legs hurt. It could have just been what some call 'growing pains,' but still I watched her carefully. Finally I noticed small, hard nodules, or bumps, beneath her skin. My stethoscope was packed and in the baggage car, but I listened to her chest as best I could without it and feared rheumatic fever. So we telegraphed ahead to the hospital at Omaha."

In my embarrassment I had started shrinking in my seat and now was about the size of a pea.

"That's where Gertie went. It was indeed rheumatic fever, which is treated with salicylate of soda and a lot of hope. She is living with a doctor's family, getting rest and good food, and I pray she will recover without major damage to her heart. Now, does that answer your questions?"

I nodded as best a pea-sized person can nod.

Miss Doctor stretched a little. "And now I have a question for you. Why do you think so badly of me? Why would you ever consider that I would abandon a child by the side of the railroad tracks?"

"It's just that you're so cold and heartless and thought us orphans a bother and . . ." I stopped. It sounded wrong even to me.

"I suppose I do seem cold and heartless compared to someone like you. And I don't have your way with children. But I do care about you, all of you." She gave me a feeble little smile and went back to humming to Lacey. I sat down in the rocker and rocked and rocked, wishing someone was humming to *me*.

All night Miss Doctor and Lacey sat there. People kept coming and going, wanting to know how Lacey was doing. Both Mr. and Mrs. Tuttle wanted to spell Miss Doctor so she could rest or eat or stretch her legs, but the lady would not have it.

I kept the fire up, brought Miss Doctor hot coffee, and between times prayed to the Virgin my mother had loved and the God my father did not believe in. I wasn't sure how much I believed, though it was worth a try. But I kept falling asleep—even for Lacey I couldn't stay awake all night.

In the morning Lacey was pinker and wasn't shivering or babbling. Miss Doctor finally put her in the rocking chair, cradled in blankets, and went out. "Keep a close eye on her," she said from the doorway, nodding toward Lacey, "and call me immediately if she . . . if . . ."

"I will," I said. I put the cat on Lacey's lap, and they snuggled together.

"Miss Doctor thinks you'll likely be okay now," I said to her, "or she wouldn't have left you."

She opened her eyes. "Hey, Ro," she said.

"Hey, Lacey."

"Your hair's all messy."

"I been sitting here all night," I said, patting my head here and there. "I ain't had time to comb it."

"That's okay. You look pretty anyway."

"Like a beautiful tree?" I asked her.

"Like a beautiful tree," she said.

I cleared my throat. "Lacey, I'm so sorry I made you run away."

"How did you do that?"

"By being mean to you."

"When?"

"In the train. Remember, I wouldn't help you keep Dumpling so you took him and ran away?"

"You *were* mean. I remember. I wanted to keep Dumpling and you wouldn't help me." Her lower lip stuck out far enough for pigeons to roost on. She crossed her arms over her chest, and Dumpling jumped down.

"I'm truly sorry, Lacey."

"And I didn't *steal* him. The conductor put Dumpling in the train, and he jumped out again. I went after him so he wouldn't get lost. Then we both got lost." She stopped pouting and smiled at the cat, who sat on the rug licking his hairy toes. "Now the train is gone and Dumpling is still here with me."

"We were so worried. You could have died out there, of cold and hunger."

"It *was* mighty cold, but the cows were warm to sleep with. And we had fresh milk to drink."

"Milk? From where?"

"From the cow. I called her Maisie."

"How did you know how to milk a cow?"

"I watched the calf."

"Well, I declare," I said. "That's pretty smart thinking." I was mighty surprised and impressed by Lacey. Maybe she was right; she wasn't feeble-minded at all. Lacey smiled again and fell asleep.

So it wasn't my fault; it wasn't Miss Doctor's fault; Lacey was safe; Dumpling was with her. I was so relieved, my feet were dancing inside Papa's boots, and my heart felt like singing a little song. I went to the window and watched the lovely, lovely snow fall on this lovely little town, and I felt almost good enough to laugh.

Lacey's ears and nose and fingertips were red and crusty from the frost, and Miss Doctor spread bacon grease on them to keep them from itching so bad. It was my job to keep Dumpling from licking off the bacon fat. I warmed gallons of milk for Lacey and watched over her when she slept if Miss Doctor wasn't there. I remembered how annoying she used to be, clinging to me and asking endless questions. How I thought she was feebleminded and dumb. How she had called me a beautiful tree. Sometimes I stroked her forehead as she slept and whispered, "Get well, Lacey. Get well."

We stayed a few days while Lacey recovered. Mrs. Tuttle came in frequently to ask Lacey how she was feeling and what she might like to eat. Mr. Tuttle bounced her on his knee when Miss Doctor wasn't looking, and ruffled her red hair. The sheriff came. "The Boss," he said, "wants to know how this little critter is feeling after her ordeal." He brought Lacey a knitted potholder made by the Boss's own two hands and threw a ball around the parlor with Joe and Sammy. The few guests in the hotel visited briefly, patted Lacey's head or mine, and went on their way. Everyone cared, but no one, it seemed, wanted to take us home.

Joe, Sammy, Lacey, and I sat by the fire one afternoon while Miss Doctor and the Tuttles paid calls on people to see if they might want an orphan. "Nobody cares a hang for orphans anyway or we'd not be orphans in the first place," said Sammy.

"Some people want orphans, just not us," I said.

"Ain't nobody nowhere wants *him!*" Joe said, and the two began scuffling again.

Lacey climbed onto my lap. "*I* want you, Rodzina. I will adopt you."

I hugged her, hard. "Thank you, Lacey, but you can't do that. You're just a little girl."

"Then *you* adopt *me*. You're not little."

"But I'm an orphan, like you. You need a *family*—a mama with a soft lap and a papa with big shoulders to carry you on. And a house and a dog and an apple tree."

"Maybe someone will want us both."

"Maybe."

"I hope they will."

To my surprise I hoped so too.

Finally Miss Doctor gave up and admitted there were no homes for us in Ogden, Utah Territory. We were all to head west again. On our last night in Ogden we had a big fancy dinner to celebrate Lacey's recovery and our departure. The sheriff came, but not the Boss. And Buster and Angus, who had helped search for Lacey. There was antelope and elk and parsnips and potatoes and two kinds of pie.

I went outside to use the outhouse. Clouds streamed across the sky, making the moonlight dance on the snow. When I returned, everyone was eating and laughing, the firelight shining on their faces. Lacey sat on Mr. Tuttle's lap. He fed bits of food to her, and she in turn fed bits to Dumpling. Joe and Sammy were making faces at each other. Mrs. Tuttle spoke softly to Miss Doctor, and the sheriff was telling a joke to Angus and Buster. And I was all alone, watching them.

I sat down again and had another bite of pie. Lacey, with her mouth full, said loudly, "This is the best night I have ever had, and I hope I never die!"

Everyone laughed and called, "Hear, hear!"

Mrs. Tuttle said, looking at Miss Doctor, "Rutherford and I have been talking. What would you think if we kept Lacey and Dumpling here with us?"

Miss Doctor smiled at her.

"Oh, yes!" shouted Lacey. "But don't you care that I'm slow?"

Mr. Tuttle stood up and swung her up onto his big shoulders. "You're not slow. The world is just too dern fast."

Lacey nodded. "Too dern fast," she said, and she rested her cheek against his big bush of hair.

# ❧ 11 ❧

# NEVADA

JOE, SAMMY, AND I were going on west with Miss Doctor—to the Boys' and Girls' Training School near San Francisco, where unwanted orphans were sent to learn trades. Sammy and Joe would be in the shoemaker's shop, Miss Doctor said; I would be trained for domestic service. I'd be a kitchen drudge—a *kopciuszek*, Mama would say. Ironing. Laundry. Sewing. Dirty pots and pans. *Probably they'll cut my hair off and make me eat mush and dry bread*, I thought. Radishes! I might as well have stayed with Peony and Oleander and saved my bottom the wear and tear of a cross-country trip. After all the time on the train, the rocking and swaying and freezing and worrying, all I would see of California was the inside of some training school.

On the day we were leaving, the sheriff came to say goodbye. He got down off his horse, spat a glob of tobacco into the snow, and came in, arranging himself on one of the overstuffed sofas. It looked like doll furniture under him. Sammy and Joe were racing around the parlor, playing tag and making noise.

"I been talkin' to the Boss," the sheriff said. "There's jist me and her at home, and lately we been feelin' the need for some livenin' up. This squirt seems likely to be livening." He reached out and grabbed Sammy with one big hand. "How about I keep him here with me?"

Sammy kicked the sheriff hard in the leg while Joe jumped onto Sammy and hung on. Why, those two would be fighting until Judgment Day!

Miss Doctor stood up and took hold of Joe. "Would you consider taking them both? They seem to be quite attached to each other."

"I don't know. The Boss said—"

"They deny it," Miss Doctor went on, "and we don't know for sure, but I think they are brothers. We don't like to separate family if we can avoid it."

Sammy shouted, "Don't be stupid. I tole you Joe ain't my brother. Joe's—"

"Shut up!" hollered Joe, kicking at Sammy.

"Joe's . . ." Sammy stopped and looked down at his feet.

"Go on, Sammy. What about Joe?" Miss Doctor asked. I was glad she did, for I was mighty curious as to where this was going. There had been a lot of interesting talk from them lately about secrets.

Sammy looked right at Joe and then at the rest of us. "Joe ain't my brother. Joe's my sister."

There was sudden silence. Sister? We were all completely discombobberated. *Sister?*

I looked at Joe. It could be, I supposed. Joe and Sammy had come late to the train and never did get washed up and buttoned into new clothes at the home like the rest of us.

Joe stood stiff. She blushed red as Mama's beet soup, stuck out her jaw, and said, "Yeah, sister. Any of youse want to make somethin' of it?"

None of us did.

"You mean you've been lying to—" Miss Doctor began, but Sammy interrupted.

"It wasn't no lie. I told the truth. Joe *ain't* my brother."

The silence went on and on while we each tried to make sense of what Sammy had said. Finally the sheriff cleared his throat, rocked on his feet, and snapped his suspenders a few times. "Well, my home is *awful* quiet," he said. "Probably take both of you to liven it up." He opened his arms and gathered them in.

Joe and Sammy smiled at each other. They actually smiled at each other. In fact, all three were grinning like Halloween pumpkins. Why, the world had not seen such a sight since Duke Ladislaus the Short united Great and Little Poland in 1314.

Sister! Imagine that. I shook my head.

So Sammy and Joe stayed in Ogden, Utah Territory, with the sheriff and the Boss. I sure would have liked to get a look at this mama who was even bigger than Sheriff Earl, but I never did.

Right around dinnertime, we said goodbye to the sheriff and Sammy and Joe at the hotel. I shook Sammy's hand and wished him good luck and hot potatoes ever after. I tried to hug Joe, but she gave me a look that would wither a cornstalk at fifty paces, so I shook her hand too.

Mr. Tuttle drove Miss Doctor and me to the station. Mrs. Tuttle and Lacey came along. On the platform, Lacey wound her arms around my neck and kissed my cheek over and over. Saying goodbye to her was as hard as I was afraid it would be. Lacey had squirreled her way into my heart. You couldn't not love someone just because you didn't want to love them.

"I will write you letters, Lacey," I said, "and

your new mama can read them to you until you learn to read for yourself."

"I'm sorry we won't be sisters," she said, "but I ain't scared or sad anymore." I hugged her and hung on for a while, humming the song Mama and Papa used to sing on my birthday: "*Sto lat*, a hundred years, may you live a hundred years." Then all the Tuttles climbed back into their wagon and drove away.

There were Indians at the depot. The men wore cotton shirts and breeches, with bright striped blankets tied around their waists; the women were so wrapped in their blankets of dark blue that all I could see of them were their moccasined feet. One boy, about the size of Mickey Dooley, had glossy black hair tied with a strip of red cloth and a tough, dangerous face. He passed close by me, and I took a good look at him.

He stared right back. His eyes were so sad, afraid, and unsure. I was surprised, but then I wasn't. There was a lot going on in all of us beneath what people could see. You'd think that after Mickey Dooley, I would have known that.

Even me. There was plenty going on inside me that no one could see. Yes, you'd think I would have learned.

I gave the boy a little friendly wave, like I would Mickey Dooley. He did not wave back.

The Indian boy and his family climbed onto the landing behind the last car on a train headed east. It would be mighty cold out there. I wished they were allowed to stay inside, where it would be a bit warmer. All they wanted was to get from one place to another, just like the rest of us, I'd wager. Miss Merlene had been right, I guessed; they'd been robbed.

So Miss Doctor and I alone would board the train for California. Seemed like I was the most unwanted orphan of all. Seeing as I had planned it that way, it wasn't right that I felt so bad about it. But I did. I could see now that some people would take orphans to care for them and not turn them into slaves. Good people like the Tuttles. And the sheriff. There were families out there for orphans, and I wanted one. I wanted what Nellie and Spud and Chester, Mickey Dooley and Lacey, Joe and Sammy had—someplace where I would belong, with a real family, people of my own who cared about me.

But it was too late. I wondered whether there were people like that in Grand Island or Cheyenne, people I didn't notice because I was too busy worrying about being sold. And now I was an orphan permanently and forever. Maybe I could . . . what? What could I do?

Miss Doctor bought our tickets from a pimply-faced boy in a bow tie who sat behind the window grille in the station waiting room.

We found an empty bench outside and sat down to wait for the westbound train.

Miss Doctor sighed a big sigh. And then another. And another. "Sister," she said. "Imagine that. A girl. You'd think I would have noticed, being a doctor, trained to observe people. I suppose I was just too caught up in my own problems to see what I should have seen."

"You think Joe will turn out all right?" I asked her. "And Sammy, Lacey, Nellie, and the others?" *And me*, I wanted to add, *what will happen to me? Will I be all right?* But I couldn't ask that out loud. "Everyone says orphans come to no good end," I added. "Even Mr. Szprot said so."

"I wouldn't pay too much attention to what Mr. Szprot said. He did his job, I suppose, but sometimes I thought his cigar knew more about children than he did."

I stared at her. Miss Doctor was full of surprises. "But was he right? Do orphans mostly come to a bad end?"

"Lots of people who start out as orphans do fine. Take Oliver Twist and David Copperfield in books by Mr. Dickens. Or Mark Twain's Tom Sawyer. And Jane Eyre, an orphan and a girl."

"Those are all in stories. Do you know of one real orphan, one real live orphan, who turned out all right?"

"I cannot think of an example at the moment."

I knew it. Even the educated Miss Doctor could not think of one happy, successful orphan.

"Don't worry so much," Miss Doctor said. "You will do well at the training school, be clothed and fed and learn a trade. The experience will be very . . . uh, beneficial. Now, I am chilled to the bone. Shall we go inside and wait by the stove?"

"No, you go. I'll stay here." Miss Doctor went inside while I walked onto the platform. I looked up the tracks and down. They stretched east and west, forward and backward, ahead and behind, like my life. Did the tracks end at the Boys' and Girls' Training School? Is that where my life would end? Where else could I go? And what would I do?

I could hear the long, hollow sound of the train whistle before I could see it coming. Suddenly there was a light, like a giant star, rushing closer and closer, and the awful *thrump*ing noise of the engine. The engine got bigger and bigger as it hurtled into the station and then, with a wheeze like it had the grippe, stopped, sparks shooting from the wheels.

Miss Doctor came out of the waiting room, and we boarded and found seats. I sat by the window and watched as we left the snowy fields of Ogden behind. The car was noisy with the sounds of quarreling and crying and the fretting of babies, and smelly with packed lunches and cigars.

At sunset we pulled into an eating station that was nothing but a shack with dirty tables and dirty waiters and dirty water. The diners were all frantic to get the waiters' attention and some of those big platters of food before the train moved on. Miss Doctor had turtle soup and tea for fifteen cents. I looked longingly at the steak others were eating, but it was fifty cents and I remembered what Miss Doctor had said about being far from rich. Instead I ordered rabbit stew and bread for ten cents, and worried as I was about my future, still I ate every bite of it.

After supper we boarded the train again and settled in. The train roared and thundered as it crossed a gorge on a huge trestle, then burst into the mountains, clinging to a narrow ledge of rock.

Finally we entered the broad, dry, rugged highlands of Nevada. We had left the territories and were back in the United States.

We rode through deserts of dirt and sagebrush. I didn't see a town or a tree or a river. Those of us on the train might have been the only living things in the whole world.

All night and all the next day we roared through wide barren plains bordered by mountain slopes. The train tracks ran straight ahead, the road beside them marked with hand-lettered signs: Dead Horse Ravine—3 miles; Greasy Neck—10 miles. Skunk Gulch—5 miles; Squibbler—20 miles; Civilization—Too Blamed Close. I grew dirtier and achier, tired of riding but afraid to reach the end of the trip. Was this California still in this *world*, or were we traveling to the moon?

# ❧ 12 ❧

# VIRGINIA CITY

IN THE DARK, the rattling and bouncing of the train was like the rhythm of a song. It soothed me but did not make me sleepy. I thought about Lacey and Joe and Sammy. They had been like my family for a while. Now they had families of their own, families who would not make them dig ditches or boil laundry. I missed them, but mostly I was worried about what would become of me.

"Miss Doctor? I'm awful unhappy about being left at this training school because no one wants me."

She was quiet for a moment. "I know how you feel," she said finally. "When I decided to become a doctor, I was discouraged by everyone. My family turned their backs on me. No physician would take me on as apprentice, and most medical schools were closed to women."

I kicked the seat in front of me a few times. I doubted that she knew how I felt. After all, she had a mama, didn't she? I stopped kicking. Did she still have a mama? I didn't know. I didn't know anything about her. But I was curious. "Why didn't they want you?"

"One dean said it was not fitting for women to know about themselves because it made them nervous." She frowned. "I was also told that too much education would leave women with monstrous brains, puny bodies, and abnormally weak digestion."

"Is that true?"

"Of course not. Do I look shrunken and sickly? The university in Michigan finally accepted me, but grudgingly. Not a day passed but somebody made me cringe, someone hurt me. I suffered frogs in my boots, blood on my chair, and laughter in the classroom whenever I sought to ask or answer a question. But I persevered."

"And now you are a real doctor." I admired her stubbornness. Why, she was just as determined on her goal as that rat we saw at the Cheyenne station.

"Yes, indeed, although most people call me Miss or Doctress, as if a woman could never be a true doctor. If I were an ax murderer or suffered from hydrophobia, I could not be more unwanted."

Unwanted. Like a stubborn, too-big orphan girl in her father's boots. Like me, on my way to a training school with other unwanted orphans, with no plans and no hope, thrown away like garbage into Bubbly Creek. I turned my face from Miss Doctor and worried myself to sleep.

The morning found us back in the clear, cold air of the mountains. At Reno station Miss Doctor and I climbed down and walked a bit to stretch our legs. "I am going in to send some telegrams," she said. "I must alert the training school that you are coming. Our train will not depart until after that one leaves for Virginia City, so you go sit on the bench by the ticket window and wait."

This was it. Miss Doctor was actually taking me to the training school, and I had no better plan for myself. My chest grew tight, so I drew myself a cup of water. There were, of course, notices pinned to the wall of the depot, and I read them as I drank:

---

### WANTED TO GO INTO THE COUNTRY,
a competent Protestant cook,
understanding the care of milk and butter.
Apply to H. James, 11 River Street, Reno.

## Madame Solanga,

CELEBRATED MEDIUM AND FORTUNETELLER,
is stopping at the Reno Queen Hotel,
where she may be consulted in any
language on matters pertaining to
business or other troubles.

## Millions of acres of LAND

in California, the Cornucopia of the
World, for sale on 10 years' credit.
No cyclones or blizzards.

## Ho for the New El Dorado!

1400 secondhand Six Shooters
and 1000 Winchester Rifles.
As the routes to riches
in Gold and Silver pass
through dangerous territory,
it is necessary that all parties
go well Armed.
Call on
THE MARVIN FIREARM COMPANY.

There were no wanted posters for Big Nose George or anyone else. One notice, bigger than the others, said in fancy lettering:

# Spinsters' Paradise!

Miners and ranchers of all ages, sizes, and
conditions seek women to share their
prosperity. Genuine ladies preferred.
Offer marriage, home, and a generous monthly
allowance. Write to Mrs. F. Stifflebean,
Virginia Palace Hotel, Virginia City, Nevada.

Stifflebean? It seemed an all-fired funny name to
me, but I did not laugh; those of us who have
Czerwinskis and Kwasniewiczes and Stelmachoskas
among their relatives know better than to laugh at
Stifflebean.

I sat as Miss Doctor had instructed me but
kicked my heels hard against the bench. Here I
had crossed nearly the whole country, only to end
up unwanted in four states and two territories.

Was I some puny, helpless girl who sat and
waited for what happened to her? No. I was big,
like a beautiful tree, and nearly grown up. I had
gotten myself off the Chicago streets and away
from Peony and Oleander and Mr. Clench; surely I
could figure some way to get myself out of this.

*Virginia City, Nevada!* I realized all of a sudden.
That notice seeking brides for miners was from

Virginia City, Nevada! That was where Miss Doctor had said this little train was going. I wondered if there were women here who were going to be brides.

A pretty woman in China-blue silk rustled by me. Was she going to wed a miner? I, too, could wear China-blue silk, have my hair up, and look pretty, if I were a bride and not an orphan.

Then like a thunderclap it hit me. Could this be the answer? Could *I* be a miner's bride? Why not? I looked older than twelve—Mrs. Clench had thought I was fifteen—and by marrying some lonely miner, I could get myself a home and a family and a monthly allowance. I would not touch the old coot Clench, but marriage to a nice man of my own choosing would be better than some training school where they would shave my head and boss me around. Miss Merlene had seemed happy enough.

I stood up and looked for the telegraph office so I could tell Miss Doctor about my idea. Then I stopped still. Miss Doctor would not think this a good plan. I knew that. I had to move quickly before she came back.

I pulled up my stockings, scratched my knees, straightened my shoulders, and approached the ticket clerk, a young man in spectacles and red suspenders. The window grille cast dark shadows across his face. "How much is a ticket to this here Virginia City?"

"Round trip or one way?"

"One way," I said confidently, for a new life awaited me at the end.

"That'll be a dollar seventy, miss," he said.

It might as well have been one million and seventy. I had no money at all. But I did have my belongings in a cardboard suitcase back in the other train. Mama said you could always call on the Virgin for help, so, in a way, I did. "Could I," I asked him, "trade a statue of the Virgin Mary, come all the way from Poland, for a one-way ticket?"

He shook his head. "Not a hundred statues. I have to deliver money to the railway, not bric-a-brac."

*Psiakrew.* Now what? I walked outside onto the platform.

"All aboard!" called a jolly-faced conductor with white chin whiskers and a nose like a tomato. People came and went, climbing on and off the train. I joined a family-looking group, hoping to be taken for one of the children, but the conductor grabbed my arm. "Your ticket, miss?"

Taking a deep breath, I looked slowly and sadly up at him. "Oh, Mr. Conductor, sir," I said in a passable little-innocent-child voice. "My old granny has already boarded the train, and I did not get to embrace her and say goodbye, and it is sure to be the last time I see her, for she is ailing. And old. And going blind. And . . ."

People were crowding up behind me, wanting to board. "All right then, little miss, scamper on up and hug your old granny," he said. "But be quick, in and out, for we leave in"—he pulled a watch from his pocket and consulted it—"three and a half minutes."

So I scampered on up, but I stayed there, hiding in the toilet compartment in the back of the car. *Please*, I thought, *let the conductor forget about me, let no one need to use the toilet, and let the train start soon.*

And then, with a rumble and a lurch, we were off. My heart did a cartwheel, something the rest of me could never do, although I had tried once when I was seven and suffered a twisted ankle and a broken finger that still hurt sometimes in the rain.

As the train gained speed, I felt fidgety and unsure. I mourned a bit for the cardboard suitcase left behind, with Mama's shawl and the Virgin and the other things to remind me of home, but there had been no time to fetch it from the California-bound train. And I had an uncomfortable feeling about leaving Miss Doctor like that. I supposed I should have left her a note or a message. How long would she wait, looking for me, before she gave up and just continued on west without me? But she never would have let me go, I told myself. And she didn't really care for me anyway. I was just her business. Maybe she would be relieved I was no longer around to annoy her.

Making myself as small as a tall person could, I came out from the toilet compartment and huddled in a seat near the back of the car. I watched the rugged hills, streams, and miles of evergreens drift past us out the window, but had to hide again whenever the conductor came in.

The other passengers settled in for the ride, unbuttoning coats, unpacking lunches, and unfolding newspapers. There were a few women—an older lady with her hair up in sausage curls, a young woman with pink cheeks and a sailor hat, a girl in a straw bonnet and ruffled shirtwaist, a black-haired girl with a parasol in her tiny hands. Were they going to be brides? They sure were pretty, I thought, and would have no trouble finding someone to marry them. Catching my reflection in the train window, I spit on my hand and smoothed down my hair a bit and crossed my legs carefully to hide the holes in the knees of my stockings.

In the seat in front of me sat a man and a woman, who stared smiling into each other's faces. She had on a walking suit of gray trimmed with fur, and he had a homburg, rich black and freshly brushed and fuzzy. Maybe that could be me and my husband-to-be, on our way to our new home and new life. At our wedding we would share bread and salt and wine, and I would never be hungry or lonely again. We would have a house and an apple tree, and Lacey could visit. And Sammy, Joe, and Mickey Dooley. And Miss Doctor. Maybe they would come at Easter and we would eat pork sausage and horseradish and decorated eggs. . . . I sighed as the man in the homburg kissed his lady's hand.

The train began a winding, twisting track that led up and down, shut in the cold, dark heart of the snowy mountains. The clouds were thick and low. On the hillsides I could see the faint green of new grass, but also the scars of pits and tunnels and heaps of dirt, rocks, and refuse.

As we raced along, I counted fenceposts. Mama

had told me that girls in Poland foretold the appearance of their future husbands by the shape of the fourteenth fencepost they passed. No matter how many times I started counting anew, the fourteenth post only predicted a short, stubby husband, worn and splintery, advertising tobacco and hog feed.

Then around another turn and we were in Virginia City. It was little for a city, even in the west. The town rose from the railroad tracks in a series of terraces hanging on the side of the mountain, each level crowded with houses and stores and saloons, churches and hotels, and some grand buildings with balconies and clock towers.

The depot was crowded with red-blanketed Indians, cowboys in big Stetson hats, flannel-clad miners, and even a few ordinary folk. But not one of them was a woman. All those people, and every one of them a man. No wonder this Mrs. Stifflebean had sent for women. No man could find a bride in this city of men. I felt a little jolt of fear. Were all those men waiting for me?

We were in Virginia City, but I did not get off the train right away. I watched the activity out the window for a bit. The lovey-dovey man and woman walked away together, her hand on his arm. I pressed my face against the glass so I could watch them as long as possible.

When I stood up to leave, the conductor blocked my way. His face was not so jolly anymore. "Here, missy, I remember you from Reno." He grabbed my shoulder. "You had no ticket. What are you doing on this train?"

I tried to twist out of his grasp. "Let me go!" I said. "You're hurting me. Let me go." I tried not to cry but could feel tears on my face and knew a blubber was coming on.

He shook me hard. "Riding without a ticket is stealing from the railroad. We put thieves in jail here."

Someone poked the conductor with her umbrella. "What are you doing to this child?" There next to us stood a tiny old lady, gray-haired and wrinkled but straight as a very short stick.

"This here girl has no ticket."

"And for that you threaten her with jail? Jail! Some men have no more sense than a chicken! Where are you from, child?"

The blubbering had started, and all I could say between gulps was, "Chicago."

"She got on in Reno. Said something about seeing her old granny," the conductor said.

"Well, and so she has. I will be her old granny and pay the few pennies for her fare from Reno and back." She held out her hand. "This is for you. I expect you to see her safely where she belongs."

The conductor took the money and tipped his hat. "Ma'am," he said.

"And you, child," the old woman said, looking up at me, "go on home. Face up to whatever it is sent you running away. Why, someone must be worried sick, a little thing like you all alone out here." She poked the conductor again and said, "Jail! And her a child. Ridiculous! Make yourself useful and help me off this train."

She was right—not about my being little, but I was a child. I knew that. I was not Miss Merlene or a lovely lady in a gray suit or a pink-cheeked woman in a sailor hat. There in the window was my reflection, a big, round twelve-year-old girl who looked like her papa, not pretty, with dirty hair and holes in her stockings. What was I thinking of? I couldn't find anyone to adopt me; who on earth would marry me?

I started to blubber again.

*Quit acting like a child*, I said to myself.

*I am a child*, I said right back.

I could not get off the train and marry a stranger. I had to grow up first.

What was I to do now? I would have to get to San Francisco on my own, for certainly Miss Doctor had gone on without me. Perhaps the station agent at Reno could telegraph the Boys' and Girls' Training School for ticket money. And if not, maybe I could just walk out into the mountains and starve to death. No one wanted me, no one would miss me.

"All aboard!" the conductor called, and the train began to fill up again for its return trip to Reno. I curled up in a seat and slept all the way.

In Reno the conductor pulled me off the train, holding tight to my arm as he marched me into the station agent's office. And there waiting was Miss Doctor, beautiful, dependable Miss Doctor!

"Rodzina!" she shouted, rushing at me and grabbing me. I had never noticed before how small she was, much shorter than I and not as big around as a walking stick, but I felt safe as I threw my arms around her and hung on.

After a moment she held me at arm's length and looked at me. "What happened to you? Where were you? Are you all right? We were just summoning the sheriff."

But I had started to cry again, and I could not answer. She led me to a bench where we just sat for a minute, me crying and her clucking.

When I finally looked up, she wiped my face with her own handkerchief. "You couldn't find me a suitable family," I said, hiccupping, "so I thought I'd go to Virginia City and marry a miner and we would *be* a family. But I'm too young to get married." I snuffled a bit more. "So I came back. Why are you still here?"

"I could not just leave without you."

"Why not? You left without Joe and Sammy and Lacey and all the others."

"That was different. They were placed with families. You were by yourself out in the wilds, lost or kidnapped or murdered by grizzly bears. How could I abandon a twelve-year-old orphan—even one as resourceful as you? I had to make sure you were all right. And it seems you were not."

"No," I said, "I guess I was not." I pressed up close to her. Tiny as she was, she felt strong and solid.

"You are but a child, Rodzina," she said in her cold, sharp voice, "and cannot just do whatever you take it in your mind to do." Laying her hand over mine, she added, "Promise me you will never do such a thing again."

"I promise," I snuffled. "Take me to the training school and leave me there until I die of unhappiness and bad food. I will not run away again. I promise." And I meant it. I had had enough of running. I wanted to be somewhere and stay there.

# ❧ 13 ❧

# CALIFORNIA

WE WAITED IN RENO for hours until finally another Central Pacific pulled in, headed for California. The station agent brought out Miss Doctor's bags and my cardboard suitcase. I had not lost everything from my old life after all. I still had the Virgin wrapped in Mama's red-and-yellow shawl, the big blue marble with a heart of fire that had belonged to Jan or Toddy—I never knew which—and the handmade card from Hulda that said "Friends 4-ever." I looked at my reflection in the window of the train. And from my papa, I had my boots and my face.

I settled down in my seat. With every whistle and chug we moved farther from Virginia City and closer to San Francisco and the Boys' and Girls' Training School.

Somewhere west of Reno we entered California. We stopped there to add another engine to the front of the train. The conductor said we were going to climb sharply now, and one engine would not be sufficient to pull the entire train.

The ascent was so steep, we were pinned back in our seats. No one stood or walked around. We all just sat. I prayed those two engines would be enough to get us up the mountains and we would not fail and fall back all the way to Omaha. Or be stranded in the mountains with nothing to eat but bear paws, elk nostrils, and snow.

We wound through forests of pine and fir, up, up, and up. Everywhere there were trees, green and vigorous, branches sprinkled with snow, some taller than the tallest Chicago buildings. There were more trees in California, I'd say, than poppyseeds in Mama's Christmas cake.

Every so often we passed through long, tall wooden tunnels, constructed, the conductor said, to keep the snow off the tracks so the trains could run. People lived and worked in these tunnels, which covered houses, stores, turntables, depots, sidings, everything. It was a fantastical underground world, one like fairies might live in or those prairie dogs I saw in Wyoming. Was that in this lifetime? It seemed so long ago.

At Summit station Miss Doctor and some of the others got out, but I did not. Only 7042 feet—that didn't seem so high to me, who had stood at 8235 at Sherman.

Then down we chugged to Sacramento, seven thousand feet in one hundred miles of twists and turns. The train rattled and swung on the sudden curves and narrow ledges of the mountain. The wheels on the cars ahead glowed red-hot like disks of flame.

In the pale light from the gas lamps I could see only shadows in the car. It was easier to talk about some things when you knew you were only a shadow. "Thank you for waiting for me," I whispered to Miss Doctor. "I was happy to see you."

"And I you."

"Really? Happy to see me?"

"Don't sound so surprised. I do have feelings. It's just that I keep them to myself. I tend to be private . . . and, yes, sometimes, I suppose somewhat—what was that you called me a while back— cold and frosty." She laughed a tiny laugh, the first I ever heard from her. "You should meet my mother. She could grow icicles in Hell."

So she wasn't an orphan. "Your mother is still alive?"

"I assume so. I have not seen or heard from her since I announced my intention to study medicine." Miss Doctor leaned back, her eyes closed and head against the seat back. "I've often imagined going home with my doctor bag, and my mother waiting on the porch, calling, 'I am so proud of you, daughter. Let's celebrate with white cake and lemonade.' But that will never happen. My mother never changes her mind."

How strange it seemed to me that the starchy Miss Doctor pretended just the way I did. "The notion that a woman should not practice medicine because she is a woman," she said softly, "is intolerable, absurd, and outdated. Yet it may defeat me."

"But you worked so hard to be a doctor."

"And doctoring is my only skill. What else could I do?"

"You could be a prigger or a hoister or a dip." I smiled at the thought.

She looked at me as if my head had fallen off. "What do you know of priggers and dips and such?"

"After Mama died, I spent some nights on the streets. There were lots of kids sleeping out there. I was with them for a while before I was grabbed and sent to the orphanage. And that's what they were: priggers and hoisters and dips. Melvin was a hoister. You know, a buzzer. File. Whiz. Wire."

She shook her head but said nothing.

"It was Melvin who told me orphanages ship orphans on trains to the west and sell them to families that want slaves."

"I never imagined you sleeping on the street or begging for food," she said. "I never knew. And you really expected to be sold?" She shook her head again. "How frightened you must have been."

"I was, but I should have known Melvin wasn't someone to believe. You can't trust hoisters. And after a while I could see for myself that not all the people who wanted orphans were just in the market for cheap servants." There was silence. "I know you tried your best for me. It's not your fault nobody wants me."

There was more silence then. I thought Miss Doctor had fallen asleep, but she said, "I had a telegram from Mr. Szprot. Herman has run away from his new home already." Hermy the Knife. He'd be back with the Plug Uglies in no time. There's no telling what is a family to some people.

Miss Doctor slept then. I sat for a long time

watching out the window, though I could see nothing but the reflection of my own face. We were getting closer and closer to San Francisco. I imagined myself walking up to the training school door, leaving Miss Doctor behind. I could see that door in my mind, plain as day, but I could not imagine what lay on the other side.

We raced through the Sacramento Valley late in the afternoon. Mountain cliffs and towering trees disappeared as the valley opened up wide and green, with plowed fields and a wonderland of flowers and blossoming trees. Could this be the same season I'd left in Chicago? The same country? I felt like Sleeping Beauty or Rip Van Winkle—I had fallen asleep in the Chicago winter and woke to a bright California spring.

The sun danced and sparkled on the windows of the train as we rode along. *Mama would like it here*, I thought. *She wouldn't be cold anymore. "Sit in the sun, Rodzina,"* she would say. *"It will put roses in your cheeks."*

And Papa? I could hear Papa saying, "This new land, so big. I think there could be a place here for a Polish poet."

California was large and empty. Surely if there was a place here for a Polish poet, there would be a place for a lady doctor. Miss Doctor would find work here, I just knew it. And I would spend my days scrubbing someone's pots and ironing someone else's starched collars, and no one would ever want me. Miss Merlene had found a way out of the laundry room, but it appeared I could not.

The train stopped for supper at Sacramento station. It was dark, but the air was soft and mild. The town smelled of flowers and the river.

We ate at a restaurant for only twenty-five cents each. There was a blue mug of daffodils on each table. Our waiters were quick and polite, but strange, with narrow eyes, long shirts, and loose trousers. Miss Doctor said they were from China. China! That was even farther away than Chicago. Or Poland.

A woman at another table called loudly, "Doctor!" Miss Doctor turned around, but the woman was waving to a portly gentleman in a straw hat. "How odd it is," I said to Miss Doctor, "to hear a man called doctor." She smiled at me.

After dinner she collected a telegram that was waiting for her at the station office, read it quickly, and put it in the pocket of her dusty suit. Back on the train we settled down for the night.

"Good night, Rodzina," said Miss Doctor, making that sound between a D and a G and a Z that I thought only Polish mouths could make. She looked at my stunned face and smiled again. "I have been practicing."

We rattled and swayed our way toward San Francisco. My thoughts were tumbling around inside me, and I tried to catch some of them. For nearly an hour I considered and wondered and, finally, swallowed twice, mentally hitched up my stockings, and spoke. "Miss Doctor, I want to say something. I want to stay with you and not go to the training school."

She opened her mouth to speak, but I kept talking. "Just listen, Miss Doctor. I have been thinking and thinking about this. It's a good idea. We are becoming used to each other, and—"

"Rodzina, I cannot—"

I was desperate enough to contradict her. "Don't say you cannot! You *can*. I do not want to go to the training school. I want to stay with you."

Miss Doctor said nothing, and my heart and my hopes began to shrivel. "Miss Doctor?" I said after a moment. "What do you think?"

She shook her head. "I would have to think very seriously about the responsibility of taking on a child, raising and supporting her by myself. And I would need to consult the placing-out agent in Chicago. It would take time."

"We don't *have* time." My voice grew sharp and whiny as I began to fear I was failing to convince her. "Tomorrow we will be in San Francisco, and the training school will swallow me like a chicken swallows a bug."

"I do not know if it would work. We have not always gotten along so well. And at times you have disliked me fiercely."

"That's because you and me, Miss Doctor, we're so different. But that could be a good thing. And in lots of ways we're alike. Maybe you don't know, but I do." I rubbed the beginnings of tears from my eyes with my fists. "We could be a family, Miss Doctor, you and me." I waited for her to say something.

Miss Doctor looked straight at me. "It's true I would miss you if you were not here. And I have been having serious doubts about leaving you in a training school." She was silent for a long while then, and I held my breath. "Perhaps we might make a success of it," she said, and my breath came out in a whoosh. "It will not be easy, Rodzina. We are both of us difficult and ornery."

Difficult and ornery? Right then I felt as easy

and obedient as chocolate pudding. Still, I knew what she meant. "But we can try?"

"Yes, we can try, both of us, very hard."

I smiled and she smiled back. Her gray eyes behind the spectacle lenses were as soft as kitten fur or the mist on the hilltops.

"Miss Doctor?"

"If we are to be a family, perhaps you should call me by my real name."

I didn't know her name. I had never troubled to find out. Hanging my head a little, I said, "I don't know what it is."

"Catriona Anabel Wellington. Not nearly as long or as elegant as yours."

"It will do. May I call you Doctor Cat?"

"You may."

"Well, then, Doctor Cat, what will you do in California? What will *we* do? Perhaps I could work at—"

She reached over and took my hand. I didn't know whether I was more surprised or happy. "The message waiting for me in Sacramento was a response to the hundreds of telegrams I have been sending throughout California. Finally. Professor Meyers at the new college in Berkeley tells me a small community is growing up around the school, and they are in need of a doctor. Even a lady doctor. We might make a home in Berkeley." She looked closely at me. "We may have to struggle some, but we will struggle together. And they have a high school there."

I smiled so big my lips hurt. I leaned up against Doctor Cat's shoulder, but I could not sleep. I was so happy, it was like music in my head.

"Edgar Allan Poe," I heard her say.

Puzzled, I looked up at her in the dim gaslight.

"Poe," she said again. "He was an orphan and a successful poet. Also the novelist Leo Tolstoy. He was an orphan too. I'm sure I can think of others if I put my mind to it."

"That won't be necessary, Doctor Cat," I said. "Two examples will do." Two orphans, two writers, and one of them a poet. And I had a family and was going to high school. Perhaps not all orphans turn out badly after all.

Early in the morning, the conductor woke us. "We're almost to Oakland station, pretty miss," he said to me.

Pretty? I turned to look at my reflection in the window of the train. No, I wasn't really pretty. I was better than pretty. I looked like my papa.

It was raining. "Just wait," the conductor said.

"A California rain is like an old woman's dance. It doesn't last very long."

And he was right. By the time we arrived at the Oakland station, the rain had stopped. And we stepped off the train into blazing California sunshine.

# PRONUNCIATION GUIDE

This is roughly how these Polish words in the story are pronounced and what they mean:

| | | |
|---|---|---|
| *chuligan* | hoo-<u>lee</u>-gan | hoodlum |
| *kapusta* | ka-<u>poos</u>-ta | cabbage |
| *kiełbasa* | kew-<u>ba</u>-sa | sausage |
| *klops* | <u>klops</u> | meatloaf, meatballs |
| *kopciuszek* | kop-<u>choo</u>-shek | slavey, drudge |
| *kopytka* | ko-<u>pit</u>-ka | potato dumpling |
| *łajdak* | <u>wy</u>-dock | villain |
| *osioł* | <u>o</u>-sho | donkey |
| *pączki* | <u>pone</u>-chkee | doughnuts |
| *pan* | <u>pahn</u> | lord, mister, master |
| *panna* | <u>pahn</u>-na | miss |
| *psiakrew* | <u>sha</u>-kref | dog's blood! (an oath) |
| *rodzina* | ro-<u>dzhee</u>-na | family |
| *sto lat* | <u>stoh</u> <u>lat</u> | a hundred years |
| *świnia* | <u>shvee</u>-nya | pig |
| *złoty* | <u>zwo</u>-tih | a unit of currency |

# AUTHOR'S NOTE

THERE REALLY WERE orphan trains. Between 1850 and 1929, nearly 250,000 poor urban children were sent west from the slums of the east and, toward the end of the century, from the midwest. The children had been living on the streets or in overcrowded orphanages. Most of them were orphans; the rest were abandoned, neglected, or sent away by desperate parents. It was thought that hard work in the clean air of the west would offer children a better chance to lead happy and productive lives.

The most famous of the "placing-out" agencies was New York's Children's Aid Society, established in 1853 by a young minister named Charles Loring Brace. He was dissatisfied with the existing options for homeless children. Children could be bound over, or indentured, to local families in exchange for their labor, a system that led to many abuses. Orphanages, a fairly recent idea, were few. Some were strict but fair, demanding much of the children but offering them food, beds, and sometimes work training. Many were unhappy places where children were lonely, frightened, and abused. Workhouses offered lodging and food to children and adults in return for work in factories or laundries. There were not enough of these institutions to house all the homeless children, and young people were put in jails merely for the crime of being homeless.

Brace developed a plan that would provide self-sufficiency and a home life to homeless children. A published summary of the work of the Children's Aid Society written in 1853 stated that "homeless waifs [found] themselves in comfortable homes, with all the boundless advantages and opportunities of the Western farmer's life about them." This was true, perhaps, for some children. Not all were so fortunate.

The Children's Aid Society was funded by private donations, churches, and charitable organizations, which paid for clothing, food, and transportation for the children as well as salaries for those who accompanied them west. The selected children—infants to adolescents of fourteen or so—were found on the streets or in institutions or were surrendered by their parents. They were scrubbed, dressed in new clothes, and put on trains headed west. There were no disabled children and none suffering from contagious or disfiguring diseases. Almost all were white and Christian, as these were thought most likely to find homes in the west.

The trip was difficult for the children, who were leaving their families, friends, and whatever homes they had known and heading to an unknown future. They were travel weary and confused. Train cars were filled with the sounds of weeping children, although many said later they were too frightened or too angry to cry.

At predetermined stops the children were lined up to be looked over. Many orphan-train riders remember feeling like cattle as prospective parents looked at their teeth and felt their limbs to make sure they were strong enough for work.

Some children were welcomed by their new families and new towns. Others were beaten, mistreated, taunted, or ignored. People were suspicious of these skinny young people with strange accents, fearing they carried "bad blood" from their unsuitable or unlucky parents. Some children drifted from home to home in an attempt to find someone who wanted them. Many ran away. Some reappeared on the streets or in the institutions they had started from.

There were attempts to keep track of orphans and their new families. Detailed records were kept of the number of children sent, their ages, where they were from, and where they were placed. No notation was kept of how successful a placement was: Were the new parents satisfied with their choices? Were the children happy? Were they ill fed or abused? Did they remain where they were placed? Only the children knew for sure. The reality of the great distances involved and the small number of agents made the Society and other placing-out agencies dependent on the benevolence of the adopting families.

The orphan trains ceased with the beginnings of the Great Depression. There were new doubts about the value of hard work for children, a decreased need for farm labor, and fewer families who could afford more mouths to feed. New social programs emphasized temporary foster care or the use of public money to allow poor families to stay together.

Some members of the last generation of orphan-train riders are now in their seventies and eighties. Their firsthand accounts of riding the trains, and lots of other information, can be found on the website of the Orphan Train Heritage Society, www.orphantrainriders.com, and many other websites. Search under "orphan trains."

The Children's Aid Society did not invent the idea of "placing out" large groups of children. In 1618 two hundred English boys, most of them orphans, were sent to Richmond, Virginia, to work on plantations there. The boys needed homes and provided cheap labor for the colony. Hundreds more followed.

In the mid-nineteenth century Britain established a system for transporting homeless children as "child migrants" to other parts of the British Empire. British policy declared that these children would prosper by learning how to farm and that hard work would build character. During the next eighty years, 100,000 "home children" were sent to Canada, Australia, New Zealand, South Africa, and the West Indies. Some even made it to the United States: in 1869 twenty-one boys were sent to Wakefield, Kansas.

In the United States, starting in the mid-nineteenth century, official policies designed to "civilize" the vanquished Native Americans included assimilating the children into white society by forcibly taking them away from the influence of their parents and sending them to boarding schools hundreds of miles—or farther—away. They suffered from homesickness, culture shock, and despair. Many of the children died at school, from diseases they had no natural immunity to.

During the years leading up to World War II, the placing-out system was used to save some children from Hitler. In 1934 Jews in Germany began the Youth Aliyah movement to rescue Jewish children. By 1948 over 30,000 young people—half of them Holocaust survivors—had been sent to Palestine from Europe and the Balkans.

From December 1938 to August 1939 the British government opened the country's borders to 10,000 children from Germany, Austria, Czechoslovakia, and Poland. This *Kindertransport*, or child transport, placed children in foster homes and institutions, with the intention of returning them to their families after the war. The horrors of the Holocaust prevented that. Very few ever saw their parents again. A website called www.kindertransport.com can give you more information and lead you to other sources, including an award-winning documentary called *Into the Arms of Strangers*.

After England entered the conflict in 1939, transportation for children from Nazi-occupied countries into England ceased. More than a million children—both British and refugees—were sent away from British cities deemed most vulnerable to Nazi bombs or invasion. Some were sent into the countryside, away from the heaviest bombing, where they were taken in by foster families, sent to orphanages, or worked on farms (the same was true in France and, later, Germany).

Thousands of children were sent to other parts of the British Commonwealth: Canada, New Zealand, Australia, and South Africa. In the chaos of war and its aftermath, the children's records were often incomplete, falsified, or lost. Children landed in foreign countries with no passports or histories. Parents sometimes could not find their children; children were informed their parents were dead. Some of the youngest never knew they had had a life before exile.

These various efforts were responsible for saving thousands of lives and offered new hope, opportunities, and families to children in real danger. Many survivors of the orphan trains and other movements feel fortunate. Others consider themselves abused and damaged. For most, however, it was a mixed experience. Siblings were often separated, and contact between them was discouraged. City children had to perform hard farm labor for which they were neither emotionally nor physically prepared. The children were "different" and sometimes unwelcome. They had to contend with jealousy and competition in their new families. Often they grew up feeling they didn't really belong anywhere. They suffered divided loyalties, wondering about their original families as they grew away from them. To survive, they had to be content with life among strangers.

Today there is much debate about what makes a family. Children do not seem to care about definitions; they just want to belong to someone.

If you wish to know more about the orphan trains, here are some places to start:

Eve Bunting. *Train to Somewhere*

Annette R. Fry. *The Orphan Trains*

Isabelle Holland. *Journey Home*

Marilyn Irvin Holt. *The Orphan Trains: Placing Out in America*

Joan Lowery Nixon. The Orphan Train series

Stephen O'Connor. *Orphan Trains: The Story of Charles Loring Brace and the Children He Saved and Failed*

Orphan Train Heritage Society of America. *Orphan Train Riders: Their Own Stories*

Michael Patrick, Evelyn Sheets, and Evelyn Trickel. *We Are a Part of History: The Story of the Orphan Trains*

Michael Patrick and Evelyn Trickel. *Orphan Trains to Missouri*

PBS Television. "The American Experience: The Orphan Trains"

Charlene Joy Talbot. *An Orphan for Nebraska*

Martha Nelson Vogt and Christine Vogt. *Searching for Home: Three Families from the Orphan Train*

Andrea Warren. *Orphan Train Rider: One Boy's True Story*

Andrea Warren. *We Rode the Orphan Trains*